IRENE TE

01:07

THIS SONG IS OURS

Irene Te

STORIES FROM
This Place is Magic

First Edition: January 2025

Library of Congress Control Number: 2024922409

ISBN:
979-8-9900566-4-0 (Paperback)
979-8-9900566-3-3 (Hardcover)
979-8-9900566-5-7 (eBook)

For my stakeholders:
Ayana, Carrie, Anne, Aly, and Charlene
(but also Marty!)

And for Joeli, because I can't live without her. I tell her
all the time, but it needs to be in print. LOVE YOU
JOEY.

Contents

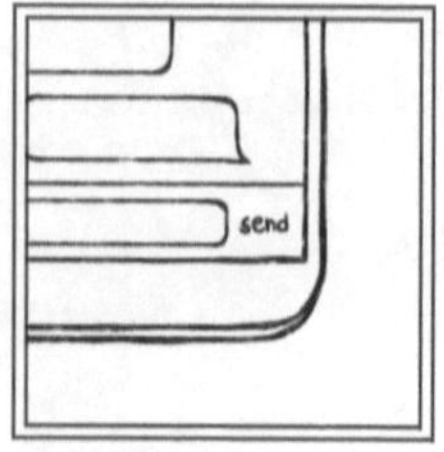

Messages exchanged between Apollo's Park Jungwoo and actress Hazel Lim on the night of the group's departure from Emerald Entertainment, timestamped June 22, 2023

@heeeyzel ✓

not yet

but you will be

@jw_0rpheus ✓

Hazel, come on

Hazel

???

Seen

The Name of the Game

Max

T HIS IS A NICE hotel. Not that Max hasn't stayed at his share of nice hotels, but their current location is a standout.

First of all, the room he's sharing with Jesse has access to a balcony facing the beach. Kei and Namgyu can use the same balcony from the adjoining suite. The lounge chairs are long enough for everyone's coltish legs to stretch freely, even if they aren't the most comfortable. Maybe they can hang out here tomorrow while they're hiding from the reporters and frenzied fans.

Second, none of his oldest brothers is on the same floor. Fucking hallelujah.

Third, there's coffee and hot cocoa available in the lobby

24/7.

Fourth, there's a boardwalk on the far end of the beach, beyond the property's bounds. Max tracks the slow turning of the Ferris wheel, the whirl of lights against the night sky, and is reminded of the tacky theme park where all three of his sisters worked part-time in the summers. They always got him in for free. Man, he misses it there.

Max is a bit sad that they'll be moved to a new safehouse in a few days. Safehouse is Denny's word for it, and since he's the best manager they've ever had, Max goes along with just about whatever he says. Plus, it's thanks to Denny that the hotel's private beach lies empty, eleven whole floors below this one. No threat of being recognized. They can sneak down there anytime they want for at least another two or three days while it's closed to the public. Something about a jellyfish invasion. Or maybe it was a sea turtle migration? Either way, Denny Han is a genius. They need to keep him around.

It's been a long night. Jess is snoring in there, so tired earlier that he even skipped his twenty-three-step skincare routine and went straight to bed. Max took an unplanned power nap himself, in the car after they told Sunshines about getting fired but not disbanding. Now it's past 4am and he's wide awake, waiting for someone to come yell at him for what he did.

Max had threatened a tabloid leak and now it's there, splashed onto the Internet for posterity. Of course someone is going to come yell at him, and soon. But which brother is on the way? Will it be Jungwoo, the injured party? Nah, that fucking coward.

Kazu seems the likeliest to appear, since he's technically their leader while Jaehwan is gone. He'll feel honor-bound to deliver a scolding. It doesn't matter to Max. He's in the mood for a brawl.

But when it's Ari who shows up, there's no yelling. At first, Max can't figure out if he's gotten off easy or if this will be much, much worse. Ever since Ari came back to them, he's been different. Still Ari but weirdly wiser, a quiet conviction smoldering beneath the surface.

Kazu would've made him run extra wind sprints. Jaehwan would've come at him like an inferno straight from the deepest part of hell. That's something Max can handle, fighting fire with fire. This updated version of Ari only regards him silently, mouth turned down in disappointment.

Okay, confirmed: this is worse. Ari's disappointment feels like cinder blocks being piled on Max's chest. He's disappointed him before — he's disappointed everyone before — but this is different. It's agony. He wants to apologize immediately. Except that Max still isn't sorry, even though conventional wisdom dictates that he should be, and he's never been very good at faking his true feelings.

"If you're planning to make me hold hands with Jungwoo at breakfast, just give up now. I won't do it. And it won't make anything better, I don't care what Jaehwan says."

"Okay," says Ari, placid as ever. Placid like a frozen lake.

"And he deserved it. And I don't regret it at all. And I never will."

Ari shakes his head. "I hope you don't regret it. You've gone above and beyond this time."

"Thanks. That was the goal." Max stares past the balcony railing, out to that point on the horizon where dark sea meets pre-dawn sky. "Has Jungwoo seen it?"

"A while ago, yeah."

"Then where is he? Don't tell me he's taking the high road. He doesn't even know where the high road is. He couldn't find the high road on Google fucking Maps to save his life."

Ari's eyes flash with something deeper than disappointment. "He's hurt, Max. Really hurt."

"Good." No way is Max admitting that this reaction from his favorite brother is cutting right to the quick.

"We've all had a rough night. This pretty much did him in."

"How the hell did Jungwoo have a rough night? What was so rough about it? 'Oh, I need to get off my ass and betray everyone again. It's so exhausting. My life is so hard.' Fucking spare me, hyung." Max hunkers down in his lounge chair, prepared to die on this hill, go down with this ship, because it's too late now anyway. "Jungwoo's pissed at me? Cool. Why doesn't he do something about it?"

"Like what, though?" Ari asks him, perplexed.

Automatically, Max replies, "Fake his own death."

"Not a solution, Max."

"Everyone says that without even trying it first."

His brother sighs. "I feel bad for him. I don't know how I'd handle this, if you did it to me."

Well, some things never change. Ari-hyung would feel bad for the executioner having to swing the axe. He'd be on the chopping block, ten seconds away from being headless, still apologizing for the inconvenience.

"Okay, one: I'd never do this to you. You're not an asshole. You'd do the right thing. Which brings me to two: Jungwoo can do the right thing. He can correct what I said. Will he? I don't think so."

"He might," says his brother. But Max picks up on the slightest bit of hesitation there, and this tells him everything he needs to know.

"He won't. You'll see."

Ari shifts in his chair, struck by an epiphany from on high. "Have you read them?"

"Read what?"

"The articles."

"Yeah, I read them. I mean, I'm the one who told the tabloids all that shit. I saw as soon as it went live."

"No, no. There's been an update since they posted the original." Ari digs out his phone. "Ah, man. I thought you already knew. This is... well, at least you're sitting down."

An update? How could there be an update so fast? Why does Max have to be sitting down for it?

While Ari loads up whatever new development he's talking about, Max rallies under the banner of logic. There was bound to be a response within the next day or so, sure. It's moving faster than expected, but that isn't necessarily a problem. After all, the damage is done. And Max is certain that the others will agree, even if they're mad at him for it: he's shot a perfect bullseye with this one.

The target was Jungwoo. The name of the game was revenge. Quick and dirty, but Max got what he came for, and Jungwoo got what he deserved. So when Ari produces the articles about this self-engineered scandal, Max is feeling absolutely fine. Content, even. The cat who caught the canary and made him pay for his crimes.

The update is at the very bottom of the original post. Max squirms a little at the headline, which blazes across the screen in bold, black letters, all caps:

> **BREAKING:**
>
> **APOLLO'S MAX LEE CONFIRMED TO BE DATING ACTRESS HAZEL LIM (UPDATED)**

This news is about him, fueled by baseless lies he personally fed to the reporters always circling Apollo like hyenas. Even so, Max wants to yell, "Gross!" at the top of his lungs.

Ari gestures at the phone. "Did it have to be this? Did it have to be Hazel?"

"Yes, it had to be Hazel! Because the ass I'm kicking belongs to Jungwoo!"

"We thought you were going to tell them Jungwoo's dating her. Kazu already drafted a denial for the press. None of us guessed you'd take it in this direction."

"I knew he'd hate seeing her name written up with someone

else's. He's such a fucking loser. And now he can't admit to anything without causing an even bigger scene. Not that he will," Max tacks on, "but it serves him right."

"It's not just someone else's name," Ari points out, the very picture of weariness. "It's yours. That's a lot worse."

"I don't need you to explain why I'm brilliant, thanks."

"Max, I think he really likes her."

"Bullshit. He doesn't really like any of them, hyung. He's just throwing spaghetti at the wall and hoping it sticks."

"He's what?" Ari glances up at him, forgetting that he's supposed to be scrolling to the updated portion of the article. "I don't know that one."

"It means Jungwoo's dumb as hell. He thinks every girl might be The One. It's destiny. It'll be a romance for the fucking ages. And the whole time, he's waiting for a sign that this new girl is his soulmate. When the sign doesn't come, he dumps her and goes back to trial and error. And the joke's on him, because soulmates aren't even a thing. They don't exist."

Ari winces at this extremely thorough analysis. On Jungwoo's behalf, he says, "Ouch."

"I'm not wrong!" Max huddles under the blanket he brought outside, fuming. He's been on the sidelines for years, watching these infatuations progress from first blush to last dance. Hazel is far from the only one his brother has pursued; when Jungwoo's not chasing down the muse, he's searching for the heroine in his mythical, fated love story. Max would sell his soul in exchange for never having to see that cycle play out again.

"Look, hyung," he says to Ari. "Do you think you met Emma-noona because the stars were aligned or some shit? Like do you think you were always supposed to meet her?"

Ari pauses. "No. I guess not. I met her because I happened to walk by and see the orange door. And I got to know her because I decided to run away. She didn't have to help me, but she did. Those were all choices that we made. It didn't just line up that way."

"Okay, so that's not destiny. That's a whole bunch of choices and like, coincidences. My point exactly. Next, would you call her your soulmate? If you say yes to that, I'll barf."

A bitter laugh. "I can't call her anything. That would be a lot to ask."

"It'll work out," Max feels compelled to say, softening his tone when he sees the look on Ari's face. "What I'm saying is, you really like her. She held your hand for eight seconds and it fucked with the wiring in your brain. We all saw it. It was so gross."

"How are you under a blanket?" Ari mutters. "It's June in California."

"Listen to me! You found this person. The way you feel about her is real. She's not the only one on the planet you might have ended up with. Maybe you'd never have met Emma-noona if you hauled ass to the airport like you were supposed to, that night. And then you wouldn't know her, and you would've missed each other completely. There was no guarantee. There never is."

"That's true."

"Jungwoo would say that you met her because you were fated to meet her. Because of like, astrology or some shit. I don't know.

And he'd say you'll have no choice but to be with this specific girl because she's the only one you could possibly end up with. But," Max concludes, triumphantly, "you could end up with her because she's the only one you want. That would be different."

Ari considers this. Unlike Max, he's never been one to run his mouth without thinking. This is another aspect in which he's stayed the same.

"I think believing in destiny helps Jungwoo feel safe," he says. "If you have this idea that someone is out there waiting for you, and you'll find them no matter what happens, then life could be a little less scary. It can go wrong in so many ways, but you're meant to find that one person. If that's the case then there's always hope."

"I don't need anyone to be waiting out there for me," sniffs Max. "I don't want to be found, myself. Got better things to do. But you — she *is* the only one you want, right? I'm right. I know I am. I saw your face when you had to say goodbye. You haven't even seen her since then, have you?"

"Why are we still talking about me?" his brother despairs.

"Yeah, yeah, okay. We're not really talking about you. We're talking about why Jungwoo will be sad about this Hazel thing for like five minutes and that's it. He's obsessed with the idea of being in love with her. He's not actually in love with her, and he's never been in love with anybody, period. That's not how it would go, with you. What you've got is real."

Ari sighs again. It's not a sigh that's easy to decipher. He could be sighing because Max is right again. He could be sighing because Max is a little shit. Either way, he finally gets back to the phone, which has gone dark during the time they've been sitting here talking.

"Max, you didn't work this out with Hazel ahead of time, did you? This isn't something you planned together? Zuzu thinks it is, but Jaehwan doesn't."

"Gross! Why would I plan it with her? And I couldn't, anyway, since I don't even have her number!"

"Man. Okay." Ari scrolls to the update, which comprises only a single, lengthy line of text. He reads this out loud for Max. "In a statement issued through her South Korean agency, MK Entertainment, actress Hazel Lim has confirmed reports that she is in a relationship with Max Lee, a member of the K-pop group Apollo."

Max bursts out laughing. He's so loud that Ari lunges forward to pop the blanket over his head. This does little to muffle the cackling.

"Hyung, please," Max wheezes. "That was like, the best prank that anyone's ever pulled on me. Nicky should take notes. I really didn't think you had it in you."

"That wasn't a prank."

He succumbs to another fit of laughter. "Like you really fucking got me, man. Holy hell."

"Max. I read that straight from the article. Hazel told the tabloids that you really are dating."

Now Max disentangles himself from the blanket, hair mussed, face growing hot in the cool sea breeze. He motions for Ari to show him the phone. Then he reads the updated portion about ten or eleven times, until the sentence fragments in his brain and the words stop making any kind of sense.

Upon returning the phone to Ari, Max wraps himself in his blanket, rises from the lounge chair, and stands at the railing. Addressing the vast expanse of the Pacific Ocean, he yells, "WHAT THE ACTUAL FUCK!"

Ari gets up. He guides Max back to the chair, then tiptoes into the hotel room to get him a glass of water. Jesse sleeps through the whole thing. Like most of Apollo, he could sleep through the end times. And that's a handy skill to have, because Max winds up hurling expletives at the ocean for at least ten more minutes.

"She confirmed that we're dating!" he rants at Ari, once he's grown tired of complaining to an impassive body of water. "There isn't anything to confirm! She was supposed to deny it! What the goddamn hell!"

True to form, Ari manages to stay calm and steady during this explosion of rage. He urges Max to have a drink of water and waits patiently while every drop goes down. Then he says, "So. I think you should give Hazel a call."

"Like hell am I calling her. I'll never call her! I don't have her number and I never will!"

"I have her number."

"Why do you have Hazel Lim's number...?"

"She lost an earring on set, back when we were filming for *Trickster*. I found it and wanted to tell her, but she was already gone for the day. Jungwoo shared the number with me."

"That's just like him, getting a girl's number in the middle of a shoot," mumbles Max. "Augh! I'm not calling her. You can't make me!"

"I'm sure Hazel's waiting for you to say something. Just call. This is a big deal. Besides, you're the one who started it."

"She can wait forever! I'm never calling. What would I even say?"

"Tell her this." And Max figures it's going to be one of Ari's deluxe apologies, the kind with groveling built in, but instead he starts singing.

This voice — Max has always understood Jungwoo's admiration of it. It's one of the few things he and that bastard can consistently agree on. Even the worst, most abominable lyrics become profound, if the lines are given to Ari. He takes Jungwoo's romantic drivel and turns it into poetry.

But this is not true when he's singing the chorus of *Wedding Dress* in Max's face, even if Max did the same thing to him like six hours ago and totally deserves it.

"Hyung!" he cuts in, kicking at Ari from his chair. "You got mean while you were gone. Goddamn!"

"Hahahaha!"

"This is serious! That's the meanest thing you've ever done to me!"

Ari laughs himself hoarser than he already was. It's a helpless belly laugh that Max has only seldom heard in the past. He's in no mood thanks to Hazel's insanity, and singing these specific lyrics to your younger brother is beyond insensitive at a time like this, but Max can't help forgiving the crime instantly.

Ari went away and came back a little different. He also came back so much happier. Everything was worth it, then.

As Ari continues laughing, Max's phone buzzes on the adjacent chair, alight with several notifications he's been ignoring. He'd like to carry on ignoring them. But he can't ask his brother to read the texts for him because Ari can't be counted on for shit right now, so he sighs and forces himself to look.

First up: Mac. Of course. The sister closest to him in age is a monster who rises at the crack of dawn. She teaches Pilates to octogenarians on Jax Beach.

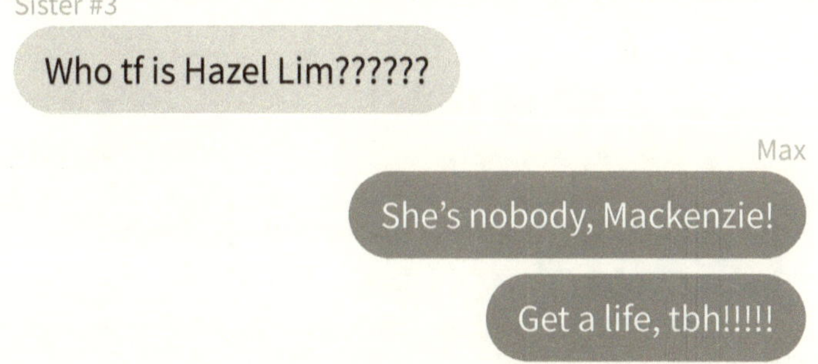

And before he's even finished firing that one off, another text comes zooming in. This one is from his eldest sister, Madison. She's a different kind of monster who can somehow juggle a husband, two children, two dogs, and her book club while still monitoring his career more closely than the paparazzi.

Sister #1

> Max, this woman is stunning. You cannot possibly be dating her. Give me names. We're suing for libel ASAP.

Max

> Shut up!

> She's the one who can't possibly be dating me! Because she isn't!

Max nurtures a fleeting hope that Mikaela didn't answer the phone when one of the other two inevitably called her, but alas, there she is as well.

Sister #2

> be honest - did u annoy her into this? u can tell me bubs

Max

> I can't tell you shit! Don't you think I learned my lesson when I was 9???

Another flurry of texts comes in, a blizzard of questions. His sisters had barely processed the news about Apollo leaving Emerald Entertainment and now he's stirred it up twice in less than twenty-four hours. Soon they'll demand that he get his ass on Zoom and provide an explanation for these antics. Max would rather take a walk into the ocean.

Sister #2

what makes this heidi person think she can just do this

max can be irritating but she's gone too far

i've never even seen her before today

Sister #3

Who is Heidi?? U mean Hazel??

Max yanks the blanket over his face. When he returns to the group text, Madison has predictably supplied a solid two-paragraph rundown of Hazel's career thus far. She's also linked to a Wikipedia entry, an IMDB page, and the official bio written by Hazel's agency. Now his sisters will know more about her than he does, since they'll probably read everything they can find and Max can't even bring himself to look.

Sister #3

Max why!!!!!

This is the same girl who was in the Trickster MV

U know?? My enemy???

Strings of emoji flood the screen. Mackenzie sends the knife four times, followed by some skulls, three angry faces, and a coffin. Max does a double take on that one. There's a coffin emoji? Since when? What the fuck?

Sister #1

> I knew she looked familiar. It's the hair color that threw me off. She had darker hair in the music video. She's cut it short since then, too.

Maddie supplies screenshots from the video in question. All of them feature Hazel with Ari, just to further provoke Mackenzie. It's the infamous scene where Hazel's character wades into a river and Ari goes after her, both of them soaked to the skin. This yields another round of knives and skulls, seven puke faces, two more coffins, plus some axes.

They filmed *Trickster* shortly after the holidays, in 2022. Max's foremost memory of the experience involves shivering in the back of a horse-drawn wagon. It was painted a shade of plum, styled to look like it belonged to a fortune teller. Hazel had smiled at him politely from the depths of a hooded cloak. The wind sliced right through his thin, unseasonal linen shirt; they had a conversation about the fact that it was goddamn fucking freezing that day. Then the cameras were rolling and it was over in one take. She was supposed to read his palm, tracing the lines to decipher his future. Max remembers that her hands were smaller than his, and unexpectedly warm.

That was the extent of it, really. His character wasn't scripted to interact with Hazel's very much. He'd estimate that the two of them shared the screen for all of ten seconds. In Apollo's music videos, the older brothers usually got the most play — Jaehwan, for example, always had some sort of arc. If there was a girl in the story, he'd be the one to win her in the end. And that happened here, too, but it was Ari's moments with Hazel that pushed the video from viral to iconic.

Sister #2

well she's w bubs now so it wasn't ari she wanted after all

Max

She's not with me! Shut up!!!

Sister #2

and anyway hannah's rly pretty but don't u guys think max is prettier

Sister #3

Omg her name is HAZEL

PLEASE Mikaela

Sister #2

why should i remember her name

> why is she important

Sister #1

> Mama wants to know if you'd like to give Hazel her rings.

Sister #3

> Ohhhhhhh that's so fucked up

> Max gets her rings bc he's the only boy???

> Tell Mama that's sooooooo much bullshit

God, this chat has gone off the rails. Now he's the one bombarding them with the knife emoji.

Max

> I DON'T WANT HER RINGS

Sister #1

> Are you sure? She's got a massive diamond. Michael didn't even get me one that size.

Sister #2

> stop pressuring bubs to marry a girl he doesn't even love!!!!

> this isn't 1882!!!!

Max doesn't stick around to read their replies. He dives under the blanket as the sky grows brighter, letting his phone clatter to the floor. Ari picks it up. He's done laughing, finally. Max suspects that a lot of the laughter was tied to the Apollo group chat, which was just starting to blow up when Mackenzie sent that first text message. At this hour, Kazu, Max, and Namgyu will be warming up for their daily workout. They're sure to be discussing Max's scandal while running demented relays across the sand. And as the others start waking up to this very first day without an agency, without contracts or any kind of schedule, the chat will just continue to explode. It's not like they've got anything else to do.

"Come on," Ari coaxes him. "Call her. Straighten this out before it gets even more complicated. I put her number in your phone while you were, uh, shouting at nature."

"Hyung, seriously?" And then, from under the blanket, Max groans, "Just leave me here. My life is over."

"It's not." More laughing, poorly disguised. "Though, you could just... fake your own death."

"Hyung!"

"I'm sorry," his brother says, and it's got to be the least apologetic Ari's ever been. He crowds next to Max on the lounge chair, his tone patient but stern. "You should say sorry, too. You didn't think about Hazel's feelings when you decided to do this. Out of nowhere, the press is reporting that she's dating someone, and it's not even the person she's really dating. Her agency wants answers. Everybody wants answers. Think about what you did to her, Max. And then call her," Ari adds, "so you can fix this."

Max remains swaddled in fabric, listening to the waves and the furious buzzing of his phone. He hasn't thought of Hazel much since they filmed that music video and he'd bet money that she's barely thought of him. It makes her response all the more baffling.

"She was supposed to deny it," he mumbles. "Why didn't she deny it?"

"I don't know. But if Hazel did that just to spite you, I'd say it was fair. I'm fine with you getting a taste of your own medicine."

At this, Max sweeps the blanket aside again. "Hyung, why are you doing this to me? Remember when you weren't mean? Fucking hell!"

"I'm not being mean. I know it feels like it, but that's not why I'm saying this stuff to you." He's quiet for a second, and then, "Max, I know you did this because of what happened with Jungwoo, the night he told the agency where I was. I know you wanted to get even, not so much for yourself but because of me. This isn't the best decision you've ever made, but I understand that it came out of loyalty. So, thank you. Not for what you did to Jungwoo and not for what you did to Hazel. But for caring about me... that part, I can't be upset about."

"You're welcome," grumbles Max. Doesn't it sound almost noble, when Ari puts it like that? And he did do it for him, because it wasn't like anybody would ever make Jungwoo pay, least of all the person he hurt the most. But if Max is being honest, most of the motivation came from something much uglier. Sure, it would've upset Jungwoo if the press caught wind of his on-again, off-again thing with Hazel. But it was worse, wasn't it, that the headlines were wrong and he'd never correct them? It only proved that Jungwoo wasn't anybody's romantic hero. He was just a coward.

And I hope it hits you like a truck, Max tells his brother, forcing an imaginary confrontation, sending only the worst vibes by telepathy. *I hope this makes it hard to keep pretending you're such a goddamn catch.* But who is he kidding? Jungwoo will feel sorry for himself, step one. Then Jungwoo will write some songs about it, step two. It's hard to believe the guy will ever change. Not for this, and maybe not for anything.

"Hey. Let's start figuring this out, okay?" Ari presses the phone into Max's hand. It won't stop buzzing. "And now you won't have to call Hazel," his brother continues, "because it looks like she's calling you."

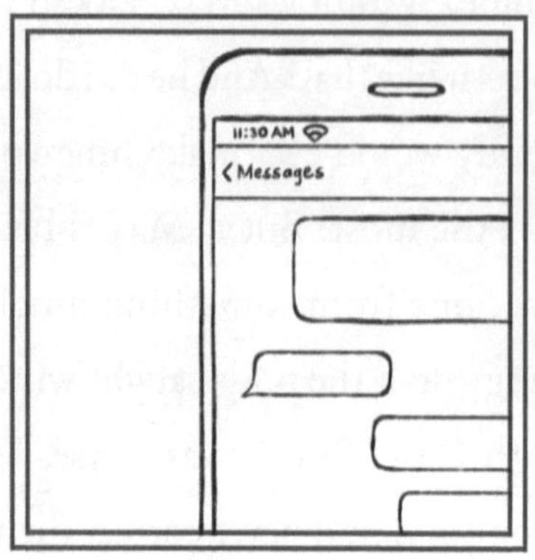

*Transcribed from the group chat shared by all
nine members of Apollo, timestamped
June 24, 2023.*

Jaehwan: So?? What happened??

Ari: I talked to him

Jaehwan: And???

Jesse: ommmggg is everybody getting a gf
now

Jesse: are we all doing it

Jesse: do i need to go get one too

Nicky: Oooooh please go get one

Jaehwan: Yes why don't you ALL go get
girlfriends!

Jaehwan: Why don't you ALL get out of my life!

Jaehwan: All purchases are FINAL!

Jaehwan: NO returns or exchanges!

Namgyu: haha but nicky did you drink my green smoothie

Namgyu: i can't find it

Kei: BIG DUMMY

Kei: You were just in my room!

Kei: IT'S IN YOUR HAND

Namgyu: awww!!! it is in my hand!!!! keiichi is the best

Ari: Sorry, Denny was asking me something

Ari: Anyway I tried talking to Max again but he won't come out of his room

Ari: He said he's staying there forever

Jesse: hyung do u mean he said he's staying there for fucking ever and he's never fucking coming out again

Namgyu: omg!!! jesse haha!!!! that was so good, you sounded just like him!!!!

Jesse: i know right!!!!

Namgyu: you're so smart, you're so good at acting!!!!

Jaehwan: Let me guess… Jungwoo won't come out of his room either.

Kei: He isn't here.

Kei: He took his guitar to the beach.

Jaehwan: Good. Maybe I'll get another 5 hit breakup songs out of him. Meanwhile, the rest of you are causing scandals or being useless. That's it. Those are the only two options.

Nicky: But why aren't you asking the really good questions, leader-nim

Nicky: Like, why aren't you asking where Ari was last night

Jesse: ommmggg u mean dad didn't tell mom what happened

Kei: Of course he didn't.

Kei: WORST

Kazu: Wait what?

Kazu: What's going on, I have to scroll back so far

Kei: Lazy!

Jesse: waaahh i'm kinda sad max isn't here to call him a deadbeat dad…

Jesse: will we ever see max hyung again…

Namgyu: awwww! max will be ok because time makes everything better! but zuzu how could you forget to tell jaehwan-hyung when it's so nice, it's the best story and i'm so happy

Kazu: What story??

Kazu: Man I have a headache

Jaehwan: ???? Try that for a straight decade and get back to me.

Nicky: But what about Ari

Nicky: You guys get so distracted

Nicky: You're lucky I always have my priorities straight

Kazu: What ABOUT Ari, why are we talking about him??

Kei: He doesn't remember. LOL

Jaehwan: ????

Jesse: ommmmggggggggggg

Jesse: ari hyung u were my nicest brother other than namgyu hyung and i'll miss u all my life

Namgyu: awwwww!!!!!!!

Nicky: Shut up so that Ari can tell us why he was in the back seat of a van with Denny's sister for twenty minutes last night

Nicky: That's my son and I deserve to know

Ari: Ah

Ari: Jaehwan-hyung, I sincerely apologize

Nicky: Yes, yes. Go on

Jaehwan: Oh, I see. So she didn't turn you down.

Jaehwan: HAHAHA

Jaehwan: HAHA HAHAHA HAHAHAHA

Jesse: waahh but when leader-hyung starts laughing doesn't that mean you die soon

Kei: It means you're already dead. Idiot!

Jaehwan: Shit, I laughed too hard and dropped my phone.

Jaehwan: Kazuhiko, you know my routing number.

Kazu: What?? How can I possibly owe you money again? What were we betting on?

Kei: I can't watch this, Grandpa's too pathetic today.

Namgyu: zuzu did drink a whole lot at the restaurant, haha! he had the best time ever!

Jesse: ommggg it's soooo funnnyyyyy he forgotttt everythinnnggggg

Jaehwan: HAHAHAHAHA

Jaehwan: Ari, text me her number. I need to make sure she agrees to my policies.

Jesse: omg omg omg ommmggggggg what will u say to pretty noona i'm so scared

Jaehwan: Just the standard stuff. Terms and conditions, return policy.

Jaehwan: Release of liability.

Kazu: Wait wait WAIT you were in the back seat of a van with WHO you were doing

WHAT

Kazu: Listen Ari can you just

Kazu: Can you remember to make good choices...

Nicky: Damn, I can't take screenshots fast enough

Ari: I think I did make a good choice

Namgyu: AWWWWW!!!!!

S.O.S.

Jeannie

THE BOSS IS ACTING weird again. But does it still count as weird if he's like that every single day? And what if he's been like that for the entire time Jeannie's known him?

She'll go investigate in a minute. First, she ducks into the pantry, where a mirror hangs on the back wall beside the apron hooks. It used to be a fixture in Janie Han's locker, long ago in the olden days of yore, like around 2011. The ghost of a sticker lingers at the bottom right. Jeannie scratches the surface with her thumbnail. It's vaguely cloud-shaped, no indication of what it might have been, but a little more of the calcified adhesive flakes off every time she picks at it.

One day in the faraway future, she'll finally succeed in

scraping the mirror clean. And then what? *I'll have to be a grown-up, I guess.* Jeannie shivers at the thought.

"Focus up, Vho," she mutters to herself. This is a big day. Wanna Waffle is reopening for the first time since the night Apollo showed up out of the blue. Denny was right to shut the place down for a while. It's turned into a pilgrimage site for Sunshines, which sounds like it would be great for business but actually isn't. Customers have to climb over a mountain of stuffed animals and steadily wilting floral bouquets just to get to the main entrance.

"Tell him you can't," she hears Denny say, every word rumbling through the kitchen like a miniature earthquake. Jeannie adjusts the orange apron tied around her waist. Then she tugs her hair out of its ponytail, runs her fingers through it, and ties it up again. She pops her head out of the pantry just as Jiyeon walks past her to grab a gallon of milk from the fridge.

"Tell who that you can't what?" Jeannie asks.

Denny materializes out of the ether, startling her so badly that she tumbles back into the pantry with a shriek. He waves a pack of paper napkins at her. "Hey, are you on the clock? What did I tell you about being nosy on company time?"

"I don't know why you think I'd remember something from last week!" she wails back at him. "I can't be expected to do that, I'm only paid a dollar above minimum wage!"

Jiyeon shuts the refrigerator door with her foot. She frowns at Denny. "You only pay the kids a dollar more than minimum wage?"

"False. And if Jeannie ever looked at her pay stubs, she'd

know that."

"But I have to look at them online, and I can never remember the password because you said I can't use anybody's birthday or any letter that's in my full name, and there needs to be like, two symbols or two capitals or something." Jeannie unwraps a piece of soda candy, taken from the supply in her apron pocket. She pops it into her mouth. "So anyway," she continues, "it's above my pay grade."

This is where the boss should declare that Jeannie is being illogical and unreasonable. He should respond with something like, "It's above your pay grade... to look up your pay grade? Are you kidding me, Vho?" But Denny is being weird today, as Jeannie noticed earlier. He doesn't even argue.

"Don't forget it's Bingo Brunch for Serene Meadows," he warns on his way out. "They'll need help with the wheelchairs."

Jiyeon looks up from the waffle batter she's stirring. "I know, Den."

"And when Mom calls after lunch —"

"Remind her to get more bananas. Uh-huh."

"If Dad asks—"

"The answer is no, he can't call the bingo numbers. He plays favorites and lets them cheat. We're not honoring any expired coupons, Jeannie and Evan are authorized for overtime, and I promise I'll stay out of the dining room so that nobody sees me." Resting the spatula against the side of the bowl, Jiyeon says, "We're fine. You should go. I thought Apollo had stuff on the schedule today. Aren't the guys waiting for you?"

"It's more like I'm waiting for them to do the next stupid thing," Denny replies. "Just keeping the reporters away is a full time job. I'll have to move them tomorrow."

"Get going, then. We'll be okay here."

But Denny only scowls harder. "Tell him you can't," he repeats. "Not today."

Jeannie feels a whine coming on. "Who is she telling? Why can't she do the thing? What is the thing?" And then it hits her. She scurries over and takes Jiyeon by the wrist so she has to stop and pay attention. "Sis. Is this about Ryan? The one I said looks just like Ari from Apollo? The one who turned out to actually *be* Ari from Apollo, except nobody ever listens to me?"

Jiyeon's cheeks flush the prettiest shade of pink that Jeannie has ever seen. It's so cute. It's the cutest thing in the known universe. Jeannie wants to shout "Bingo!" at the top of her lungs just like the little old ladies do when they come in for their weekly game. She doesn't get to react, though, because Denny barks out her name in terrifying drill sergeant tones.

"Vho, come out here. I've got a job for you."

"No!" Jeannie gasps. "Boss, I have a job! This is my job, I don't need any other jobs."

"Insubordination," he thunders back. The door slams. Jeannie trudges after him. See, she's right about this too. Denny's being super, ultra weird today. First, the music in the dining room. Second, the binoculars he left by the register. Now he's assigning her a mission?

Normally, Denny knows better than to give Jeannie

additional duties. It's taken years, but she's managed to impress upon her employer that she isn't built for complex tasks. Jeannie's skill set: matching boba drinks to waffle toppings, guessing her brand new co-worker is a K-pop idol, and playing Monopoly with the Lemon Grove community council on Thursday afternoons. But now she's being forced to grow up, go outdoors, and accept responsibilities she never bargained for. How can Denny do this to her? She's getting older, sure, but she's still a baby—

"Don't move."

Jeannie swallows her soda candy, a grape-flavored lump that lodges in her craw. As instructed, she freezes in place. How did she fail to notice the Denny-shaped shadow obstructing the sunlight here? Rookie mistake!

"There. Do you see?"

She conducts a frantic scan of her surroundings. What is he talking about? What does he mean? But then Jeannie spots them: two girls kitted out in pastels, power-walking across the street. Their twiggy arms and legs have been burnished to a beautiful tan by a summer of golf tournaments and sleep-away surf camp. One has her hair twisted into a thick braid. The other has opted for a ponytail anchored by a giant bow. That's Steph, Jeannie decides. And the other, in the big striped t-shirt, is Sienna.

It's fortunate they stopped dressing alike. Jeannie would rather retake her trigonometry final with an abacus than tell the Hong twins apart. She struggled to do this when they were in kindergarten and continues to struggle now that they're in sixth grade. Or is it seventh? Are they that old?

Jeannie gulps down some air. Is *she* that old?

Mastering the nausea, she watches Steph and Sienna greet some acquaintances from school. They smile and wave like robot beauty queens, matching sets of braces flashing as they get in line with the rest of the crowd outside Wanna Waffle. Well, of course. She should've expected this. The twins are card-carrying Sunshines and this is now a sacred site for all the looniest, most hardcore Apollo fans in the state.

"Right on time," Denny says, tracking their movements through narrowed eyes. "The intel was accurate."

Jeannie groans. "I liked it better when they were boycotting us. They should go back to the snobby donut place where they belong. Can't we just ban them from the premises?"

"Nope. Politics. Arthur Senior is on the governing board at the business association. We could use his vote when they decide who wins at the banquet this year."

"So what? He can't possibly like us anymore! Sis and Arthur Junior broke up twice already. And does he know that she turned down a proposal, too?"

Denny crosses his arms. "Matrimony," he replies, "is inadvisable at the age of thirteen. Also, it's against the law. Yeonnie made the right call."

"Yeah! Obviously!" Jeannie crosses her arms as well. "They'll see her and start talking about Arthur. Best uncle ever, he's their favorite, she should give him another chance, blah blah."

"They're not here to talk about Arthur." Oh god, he sounds ominous. And then it just gets worse, because Denny says, "Those two have some... information. I got that from a reliable source."

"Information...?"

Denny goes from easy breezy to gale-force winds in less than a millisecond. "Vho, drop the simpleton act and keep up with me here."

"No way," she protests. "It's not an act. I *am* a simpleton. That's why my life is awesome, okay?"

"What kind of fake simpleton graduates with a 4.26 GPA?" Denny counters, nostrils flaring. "Your life is awesome because you make a killing on Bingo Brunch day, even when you have to split the tip money with Evan. Now, quit stalling and do the math: who was at Lowell's last Saturday around 7:45, right when Hong One and Hong Two were picking up a bunch of fruit trays with their mom?"

The grocery store. Last Saturday. 7:45-ish. Jeannie opens on weekends, and Evan would've left for his aquarium job around 6:30, leaving Uncle or Auntie to do the Sunday restock. Jiyeon's been around a lot more lately, so she might have gone too. But Ryan was still at work that day... Mrs. Garza's exchange student cried all over him at lunchtime...

"Oh, shit," whispers Jeannie. "They saw Sis being all cozy at the grocery store with Ari from Apollo!"

Denny's eyebrows shoot up so high that they ought to be singed by the molten surface of the sun. "Cozy?"

"Boss, I'm not saying they were like, making out in one of the aisles—"

"*Making out?*"

"Who's playing the simpleton card now?" Jeannie fumes at him. "Ari's no Jaehwan, but he's still hot. Not to me, I'll pass on that age gap romance stuff, but I don't see why Sis would waste the opportunity if it came up."

"Zero opportunities came up," Denny clarifies, forcefully. As soon as his blood pressure has gone down, he carries on. "The twins saw Ryan buying her something. Noona made big goo-goo eyes over it, whatever it was. And see, this wouldn't be an issue if they didn't need to wait around for Dad. He forgot to buy the oats I put on the list. Why do I even bother making him a list? Happens every time."

Jeannie isn't listening. Now that she's been bullied into actual cognition, she sees that there's a problem here. Ryan Kim turned out to be a member of Apollo, which means that Jiyeon is dating an idol, which means she'll be eviscerated by the fans as soon as they find out. And if those annoying twins breathe even a single word of what they saw last weekend, this could blow up faster than Auntie Lizzie's highway driving speeds.

"Oh, shit," she whispers for the second time. "No, no, no. That can't happen!"

Denny throws his hands up, exasperated. "That's what I'm saying! You'll have to deal with it, and you'll have to deal with it on your own." He points at his phone. It buzzes with notifications. "Eagle just landed," he tells her, cryptic as ever. "I should've been at the hotel fifteen minutes ago. Won't be back here 'til tomorrow night at the earliest, especially if I have to move these hooligans to a new safehouse."

Her head is exploding with calculations. It's horrible. She needs a nap. Even so, she keeps a wary eye on the twins as they chat with their buddies in line. "How much have they blabbed," she asks Denny, "and where did they blab it? Social media? Sunday dinner with Gramps? Please say they didn't post it on the Sunshine Fan Cafe."

"They've been quiet so far," Denny grunts in reply. "Enemy movements suggest an intent to use this as leverage."

"Leverage? Hong A and Hong B are into blackmail now?" They deserve to get pummeled. Jeannie will arrange it personally, just as soon as she's had at least three cups of coffee. Her knees feel like jelly and the fatigue is unreal. "Right," she mutters, wondering where she'll find the energy when mere caffeine could never be enough. "I'll take care of it, Boss."

Denny gives a grunt of approval. "Godspeed, Vho." He puts his sunglasses on. "We're playing hardball. Remember what I taught you, yeah? Don't lose your head when you get in there."

Jeannie calls Evan from the back stoop while Denny gets into his SUV and drives away. She doesn't get an answer until she's called three times in a row. He always hopes the person on the line will just give up.

"Evan," she barks into the receiver, getting only crickets in response. "EVAN."

"What?"

Jeannie sighs, rolling her eyes at the same time. This is the only kind of multitasking she's willing to pursue, most days. "Did you leave yet?"

"No."

"Great. Good." Jeannie allocates some more energy into getting her shit together. "Go next door," she tells him, "get my mom to let you in, and grab the red box with the Christmas cookies on the front. In my room, okay? You know which one I mean. Then you need to bring it here, and you need to bring it fast."

"Huh? Why?"

"Just do it! I can't explain right now. We have a situation."

The line falls silent. Then, Evan hangs up on her.

Jeannie resists the urge to kick her legs and stamp her feet like a toddler. They can't both be toddlers! Since he won't pick up again, she leaves him a voicemail. Just two words: Code Violet. Then she texts it to him, too. Seven times in a row.

Evan calls back almost instantaneously. All he says is, "No."

"Yes! And you have to help me when there's a situation. It's in the rules, there was a blood pact and everything."

"But I'm so tired," he argues. "It was Whale Shark Week at the museum, and then I helped Uncle Joey shovel teddy bears into a wheelbarrow until really late last night, so I can't cope with this much stress until I've had some recovery days—"

"Blood pact," Jeannie shrills at him.

"We were eight years old, Jee. And it was fake blood."

"Of course it was fake blood. It would be so nasty to use real blood, who does that?"

"I can't handle a Code Violet right now," Evan whines.

"I can't either," Jeannie whines right back at him. "I can't handle it ever!"

Evan tries one more time. "How do you even know that it's a Code Violet? Maybe it isn't. We've had false alarms. Or maybe it's something else, and then it wouldn't be our problem."

Alright. Fine. Denny was right; this is hardball. "Evan, the boss was playing ABBA in the dining room when I got here."

She hears some muffled swearing. The panic in his tone ratchets up by a thousand degrees. "ABBA? Like... *Mamma Mia*, or...?"

"Worse. It was *Knowing Me, Knowing You*. And then it looped back to *SOS*."

He gives up after that, because now there's no question that this is a Code Violet. They both know all the codes and protocols by heart: red for home invasions, blue for creepy stalkers, green for any and all types of infestations (invertebrates or otherwise), and orange— well, Jeannie would be thrilled to never see another Code Orange in this lifetime. But even that is better than a Code Violet, so she can't really blame Evan for freaking out.

When Jeannie stalks into the dining room, Jiyeon and Uncle Joey have just finished pulling down all the chairs. Denny's ABBA playlist is still going strong, filtering through the dining room speakers like the soundtrack to her own personal apocalypse. She flinches at the sound. Maybe other people hear tragic classical music when they imagine the world ending. Thanks to Denny Han, Jeannie's visions of doomsday always unfold to the tune of some Swedish pop stars singing about dancing queens.

Jiyeon gets it, too. She's standing by the big front window, head tilted to the side, listening as the Swedes sing about a guy named Fernando. She gives Jeannie a worried smile. "Denny's going through it, huh? It's worse than I thought."

"He was too stressed to play Rainy Cafe Jazz today." *Same,* thinks Jeannie. *Same, same, same.* "And he's bad at being away from the shop."

"It's good for him," says Jiyeon. "Denny likes helping Eunjae and his brothers."

Jeannie agrees, but she has bigger fish to fry. She gives Jiyeon a hug, clinging to her like the world is ending for real. "Are you okay, though?"

There's a bit of a pause. Maybe Jiyeon just wasn't prepared for the question, or maybe she has to think about it. "I'm okay," she replies, hugging Jeannie back. "More than okay."

"Because of Ryan?"

"Well. Just a little."

"But are you sure you really want to be in a forbidden romance right now?"

Jiyeon laughs. "Is that what we're calling it?"

"That's what it is," Jeannie exclaims, taking a step back so she can grab Jiyeon by the shoulders and shake her. "I like Ryan, don't get me wrong. It's not his fault that he'll never be Jaehwan. But his fans are going to be *so* mad, and they'll never forgive you, and oh my god your kids are going to be *so* cute, but is he worth all the suffering?"

Without a second thought, Jiyeon says, "Yes."

Jeannie takes this in. "Fine, I respect your choice. Last question: what did Ryan buy you at the grocery store?"

"How do you know about that…?"

"Resources. I know a guy. Answer the question!"

"A trophy," says Jiyeon. "Just a tiny one, filled with candy. They had them at the checklanes." She smiles. "It was sweet. And he was excited to find it."

Wow, okay. Six hundred million points for him, then. Jiyeon was the only one at Olivia's without any trophies because Olivia sucks. Jeannie drags a hand down her face. "That's so cute. You guys are so cute! I might throw up!"

"Please don't throw up, Jeannie."

She's not, she can get a grip, but gosh! Why couldn't Ryan Kim just be Ryan Kim? It would be a lot easier. Jeannie wouldn't have to intervene. She could referee at Bingo Brunch, rake in the tips, and just be glad that someone she loves has a new reason to be happy.

"I've got you, Sis," she says, resigned. "I'll make sure that you and Ryan-Ari-oppa-saranghae live happily ever after. I don't expect to survive, but if I do, I'm going to sleep for twelve hours straight. I'll be in the pantry. Nobody is allowed to wake me up."

"Oh, goodness. Okay. Do I want to know?"

"No. You don't."

Evan arrives then, only thirty-three seconds off schedule. Panting, he shoves a red holiday tin at Jeannie, who takes it from him and begins summoning the strength to proceed with the mission. She can't fail. The boss is counting on her, and the fate of Jiyeon's secret celebrity romance is at stake. Jeannie has to squash those twins. She has to squash them like bugs.

Uncle Joey bustles in. Shooing Jiyeon into the kitchen, he flips the sign from 'CLOSED' to 'OPEN.' Everyone takes up their places as the restaurant floods with people. Some of them are regulars, a few appear to be reporters, but the majority are Apollo fans. They ogle everything, running their fingers over the backs of chairs, snapping photos of every surface that the boys might have touched while they were here. Jeannie waves them away from the booth she's claimed. She's ready and waiting when Evan seats the enemy agents across from her, just like she ordered.

"Sienna," she says, holding the cookie tin in her lap. "Stephanie."

Coolly, the twins assess her from the other side of the booth. "Jeannette," they greet her in unison. The creepiness! The audacity!

Sienna studies a laminated copy of the menu. It's an act. They've both been eating here since they were toddlers with a grand total of six teeth between them. "What's with the music?" Like Jeannie was alive in 1974! As if she'd have any idea about songs from the late 1900s!

"Where's Emma?" Steph inquires, cutting right to the chase. "Can we say hi?"

Jeannie can cut right to the chase, too. She plunks the red box on the table. "*Jiyeon* is busy. She's never marrying your precious Uncle Arthur and you're never telling anybody what you saw at Lowell's on the evening of June 17, 2023."

What follows is a bout of synchronized glaring. "You can't tell us what to do. You're not our babysitter anymore."

"Insubordination. And don't blame me for the fact that you got too old for a babysitter. That's literally not my problem. No one told you to start aging."

Jeannie takes hold of the cookie tin, prying up the lid to reveal its contents: her entire stash of K-pop photo cards, collected over a period of five years. Multiple groups are represented. She has all of Apollo bundled into a zip bag. This is the zenith of Jeannie's organizational system. Who has the energy after spending so much money to collect these in the first place?

Hong A and Hong B stare at these treasures with longing. Their admiration morphs into horror when Jeannie plucks a card out of the Apollo stack and rips it in half. *Sorry, Kazu. This is a Code Violet.*

Sienna shrieks. "Oh my god! You're insane!"

Jeannie shreds another photo card. The twins stare at her as if she's committed first degree murder. Her hands are trembling, but she selects the next sacrifice with steely composure, hoping it won't be Jaehwan.

"We weren't really going to tell anyone about it," Steph blurts out. "We just wanted Emma to help us."

"Help you with what?"

"Meeting them! We just want to meet Apollo! She knows them, she could arrange it—"

Rip, rip. Jesse's photo flutters to the tabletop in two pieces. "Not happening. Give up."

Steph puts her head down on the table in despair. If Jeannie remembers correctly, Jesse is her favorite. That was more of an accident than a stroke of tactical genius. She'll use real strategy now. She locks eyes with the only Hong twin left upright. "Promise that you won't blab," Jeannie says, taking up a photo of Max, "or your bias gets it."

Whimpering ensues. Sienna argues, in vain, that this photo card is sold out everywhere. She's never even been able to find it on eBay. Jeannie shows her no mercy. She moves as if to rip this one as well, but then Sienna emits the most horrendous sound, a cross between ten balloons squealing and the screech of tires on pavement. "We won't say anything! We'll leave Emma alone! Just... just don't hurt him! He's already getting so much hate because of that actress right now!"

Jeannie stares her down. She puts Max's picture on the table, grabs some napkins, and offers the pen she keeps clipped to her apron. "I want it in writing. One copy from both of you, signed." She leans back against the booth's vinyl upholstery. Oh, that was awful. It aged her at least ten years. But it's over now, with minimal casualties.

Wearily, she sets the lid back on the cookie tin. "Write this at the bottom: *Jeannie Vho deserves a nap.*"

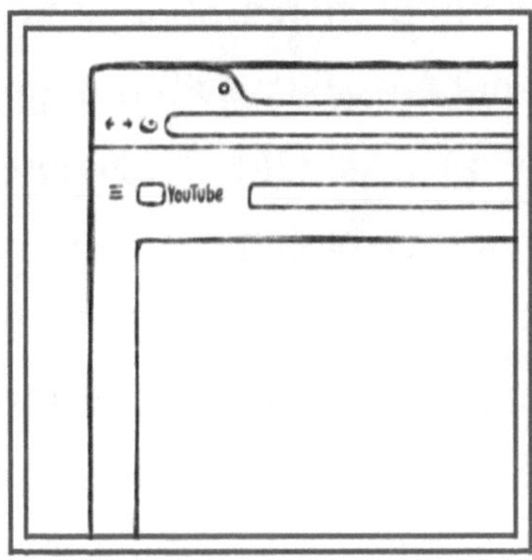

Assembled from footage recorded by fans during Apollo's second world tour, Spring 2022.

Sunshines who invested in the VIP ticket tier have piled in for sound check. Inside Apollo's Chicago concert venue, an echoing space that seats nearly twenty thousand, the members run through their set list. An Emerald staffer snaps photos for social media. And there, in the wings: Apollo's mascot, Sunny!

A pudgy ball of fire on legs, Sunny has a round head wreathed in rays of curling orange flame. His eyes are large, unblinking, and full of stars. The smile on his face never wavers. Draped in a toga, he scampers onto the stage with both stubby arms full of merch. Sunny commences tossing these items to eager fans. Gifts sail through the air. His aim could use some work... Kei takes a balled-up t-shirt to the face, and Jesse endures a brief meteor shower of towel rolls. Sunny covers his grinning mouth with both paws. Oops!

When he runs out of souvenirs to throw, the mascot bounces into the audience. He dances with Sunshines and poses for selfies. Every time Namgyu opens his mouth, Sunny makes an exaggerated show of covering his ears. At one point, he even collapses in the aisle, throwing a silent tantrum. But even these diversions can only occupy him for a finite amount of time. Sunny eventually returns to the stage. The Apollo members give him wide berth. Jungwoo doesn't dodge fast enough and ends up singing his lines while holding Sunny's enormous paw. He flinches at every move the mascot makes.

The song changes. Sunny grows bored with Jungwoo and sets his sights on Max, who stands with Ari some yards away. Max tries to maneuver them both out of range, but his brother is busy with the gorgeous, soaring verses of a Jewell song that the group will cover tonight in honor of their agency's founders. *When You're Here* is one of his all-time favorites. Sunny exploits this lapse in vigilance, wedging himself between the two members.

The creature's malign presence causes Ari to sing slightly off-key. This just about never happens; it's common knowledge among Sunshines that Apollo's lead vocal began lessons when he was six or seven years old. We hear some expressions of concern. Then the camera zooms in on Max pinning Sunny with the most acrid, venomous glare in his repertoire. "Oh no," says the fan holding this phone. "Not the king of the Ari stans!" Everyone nearby starts laughing.

Max isn't laughing. He performs the rest of the song while actively trying to edge Sunny away from his brother. And if the bastard topples off the stage, who would even be sorry? But as Max comes forward to deliver his part of the next number, the mascot detects an opportunity. Sunny stretches his leg as if to trip him. Max notices and steps over the leg with palpable contempt. The leg isn't there anymore, though. It was only a clever misdirection. His enemy gives him a thumbs up, then trips Ari instead.

Nicky lunges forward to help Ari regain his balance. He takes a moment to clap for the mascot, who sketches a bow... and headbutts him. But gently! Playfully. He's so fluffy! No harm done. Professionals to the core, the rest of the group carries on with the performance. Nicky lays down on the ground, wiped out by the hilarity.

This is, however, a turning point in the war. Max and Sunny spiral into a toxic vendetta that spans the remainder of the tour. In Dallas, the mascot moves as if to swipe at Max with his soft, plush claws. He pivots before impact, swatting an unsuspecting Ari on the nose. Max empties an entire water bottle over Sunny's head during the encore in Las Vegas; Sunny then steals all of Ari's water bottles in Seattle, whisking them away before his victim can take even one tiny sip.

"Who the heck is in that freaking costume?" Max is overheard yelling on the final night in Los Angeles. He never curses if he knows that cameras are rolling, and this particular concert is being filmed for the DVD release. Sunny responds by twirling Ari around the stage, perhaps a hair too close to a gout of fire. It's programmed to go off while the group performs *Break Point*. Max stares in horror through a shower of sparks. Sunny blows him a kiss.

Who is in that costume? Will we ever know?

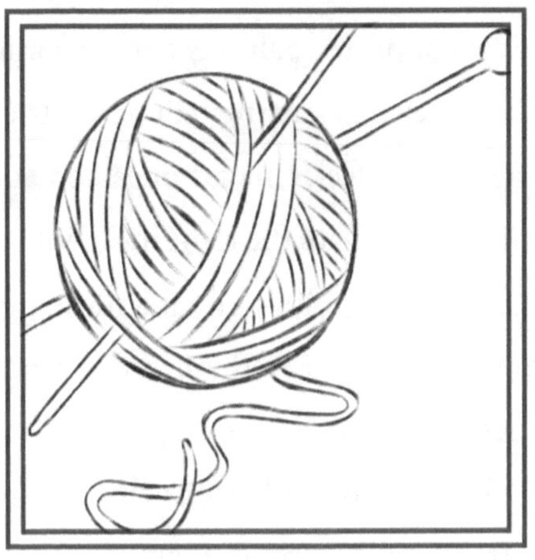

True Story

Nicky

"**S**ON," HIS FATHER OFTEN says on the phone, "why can't you just leave it alone this time?"

Well, where's the fun in that?

Every surface in this hotel is shiny. The lobby bristles with glass and faceted crystal, and as Nicky endeavors to keep his gaze tilted down, he's greeted by the absurdity of his reflection in the polished floor. He hoots at the sight. Wow, he's outdone himself this time. What an outfit. What a faithful reproduction. This is bound to be successful, a shoo-in for the *Nicky's Greatest Hits* countdown. He expects a trophy when he's done. They can find him swimming victory laps in the hotel's infinity pool.

Nicky keeps walking until he finds an alcove that suits his

purposes, tucked away into a corner. Once he sees this, he shuffles over in his pilfered platform slides. It's a good spot. Sort of hidden, sort of not. The row of potted palms generates a mirage of privacy and seclusion. Nicky claims an armchair and settles in to wait. It shouldn't be long. He can feel it in his bones: someone's onto him. They're just trying to calculate the right moment to approach.

No rush, he thinks. Apollo's on sabbatical. They don't have anywhere to be until sometime in the afternoon, and just think of all those hours between now and then. How else is he supposed to fill them? Surely Denny won't object to this creative use of time. Isn't this a country that values productivity?

The bank of tall, narrow windows faces a courtyard dappled in sunlight. Birdsong threads through the patio doors, along with occasional whiffs of sunscreen and salt breeze. Nicky counts three reporters skulking along the path. There's another by the pool gate. Each one is dressed like a standard issue tourist, but he has a decade's worth of experience. He can tell right away that they're with the media.

It's funny how quickly these goons made it past security and onto the hotel grounds. Denny hasn't even been gone a full two hours yet. While the cat's away, the mice will do anything for an interview. When will they get the ball rolling? Maybe he's not radiating enough of a scandalous aura. Nicky sinks into the cushions, but not before throwing a furtive glance over his shoulder first. He repeats this maneuver a few times. And he corrects his posture too, remembering to round his shoulders and fold his spine into a slouch. This doesn't line up with Nicky's brand, but it's vital to stay in character from start to finish.

He scrolls through Instagram on the phone he brought downstairs with him, looking over all the fresh Apollo conspiracy theories that have cropped up overnight. Unsurprisingly, he and his brothers have become the subject of several trending hashtags. His favorite is #apollocalypse. Nicky dives into the comments, snickering to himself here and there. Sunshines are in shock, Sunshines are in mourning, Sunshines have died of joy and gone straight to heaven. Emotions are high all around.

The Internet is also rife with rumors of where Apollo is headed next. Some are speculating that they'll go to another, even bigger agency. Others think the group will start an agency themselves. In the midst of all this noise, elated Ari fans can't stop yelling that he's a lawyer now, and Max fans are rioting in the streets over his relationship status. Most Sunshines are celebrating the break from Emerald Entertainment. Of course, there are voices declaring dissent at the same time.

Nine years without a single major scandal. Nicky can't believe they've taken this long to manage it. And you know what? This is the life. He has to admit that things had gotten pretty boring. It hasn't been this much fun in ages. Never mind that these shorts are ugly as sin, and they don't match the Jeju airport tee or the billowing plaid button-down thrown over it. Damned if it isn't a comfortable outfit. Definitely perfect for spectating on the fallout of his brothers' decisions. Nicky might just borrow the getup forever. The only thing missing is a popcorn bucket to go with it.

A text message comes in. He makes note of the sender, eyebrows dancing. And yet, he refrains from reading it. The code of honor is fast and loose, but it's there. "If you squint," Jaehwan would say. Imagining leader-nim's murder smile has a sobering effect. Just for two seconds, though. It doesn't stick.

When the first reporter finally comes over, Nicky is more than ready. He freezes, mouth rounded into an O. Then he scrambles out of the chair. The reporter scurries forward to stop him.

"Please, just a few questions," the guy says in English. Then he switches to passable Korean, racing to introduce himself and the magazine he works for. Well, he calls it a magazine. Nicky's pretty sure that's a tabloid.

"Sorry, but I have to go," he replies, positioning himself to flee. He tugs his hat down so that it's harder to get a good look at his face.

"Just three questions! Two questions! And then I'll let you go, I swear. I'm Kyle, by the way." The reporter whisks a business card out of his shirt pocket and hands it to Nicky. "You're a member of Apollo, right?"

"Ah... yes."

"Which one? If you could give me your name and just confirm—"

So he didn't do any research before showing up here. Excellent. "My name is Ari," Nicky replies, straight-faced, zero hesitation. "I really can't talk right now, though. No comment." For good measure, he apologizes again, in English this time.

He can't quite mimic the Australian accent, but it's not like Kyle would notice anyway. Such subtleties would be lost on this audience.

"Look, just think of your fans, Ari. Don't they deserve to know how you're doing?"

They always know how we're doing. And what we're doing, and where. That's what Nicky wants to say in reply, but he keeps this to himself. It's time for the second part of his project. He looks to the left and to the right, pretending he hasn't clocked the other reporters lurking on the periphery. "We belong to our fans. And we already made an official statement."

"Right, right. But you could think of this as an unofficial statement. Just you, talking to your fans, making it feel like more of a one-on-one." Kyle goes for what he believes to be a winning smile. "I just want to get your real, honest words out there. And you don't have an agency anymore, so it's not like they'll be speaking for you."

Nicky nods at this. "We can speak for ourselves now."

"Exactly! So how about it?"

Wringing his hands for show, because it seems like an Ari thing to do, Nicky says, "Okay. I guess I could talk for a while. No photos. And I have some questions for you, too."

"Okay, yeah. I'd be happy to help, man."

Nicky forgets about acting. Much to Kyle's chagrin, he rounds up all the reporters he can find in the courtyard. For a straight twenty minutes, he has them riveted. Absolutely enthralled. It doesn't last, though. Not because he can't hold their attention; Nicky's monologue contains a mesmerizing mix of drama, hyperbole, and outright falsehoods. His version of events is fantastic, a real page-turner. It's just too bad that this magnum opus is interrupted by the return of Denny Han.

His arrival has the impact of a hurricane making landfall. And even though all he does is confiscate three notepads and an old school tape recorder, the reporters cry uncle right away. Left behind, Nicky stares after them in disappointment. What, that's it? No one even threatened strong legal action yet.

In the elevator, Denny reads the reporters' notes. His expression is flat, neutral, impassive. Nicky sulks for about two floors and then realizes they're heading down instead of up. This piques his interest. Where are they going? Will he be marched into a bleak holding cell? Will he be interrogated for the next six hours?

These experiences would be new and novel. Nicky cheers up a little. Perhaps his morning can be salvaged after all.

He follows Denny out of the elevator and into a breezeway connecting the hotel to an adjacent parking garage. On the far end is a rectangle of flawless blue: the ocean, beckoning from beyond a stretch of sand. The beach is empty because of an alleged shark sighting in the shallows, reported by Denny to all the necessary authorities. Or was it an underwater naval training exercise?

Voices echo in the breezeway, high-pitched and excitable. Children. Nicky guesses there must be around ten of them, corralled onto a patio paved in flagstones and strewn with sand. Perched on benches, the children swing their salt-encrusted legs and chatter amongst themselves. Half have been daubed with splotches of paint. According to a sign mounted on the wall, this is some kind of day camp for the hotel's youngest guests. It appears that the kids are supposed to be manufacturing all manner of friendship bracelets and hand-woven coasters while their parents are out golfing, shopping, seeing the sights.

Are these products sold at a profit? What a scheme. He should invest in something similar, 60/40 and they provide their own materials.

Denny exchanges brief pleasantries with the two employees in charge. Both are young, in college maybe, and neither seems fully awake. They yawn over their paper cups of coffee. "Grab whatever you want," says the more alert of the two. "We've got plenty of supplies." Eyeing Nicky, the girl asks, "Dropping off or stay-and-play?"

"We'll stick around," says Denny.

"Sure. As long as the camper is, err, supervised."

A snort. "Oh, he'll be supervised, alright. Might take some of this stuff to-go, too."

"Sounds good." She glances at Nicky again. "Isn't this…?"

"Cool it, Mendoza. You didn't see him, you didn't see me, and nothing noteworthy happened all day. Understood?"

"Y-yeah. Of course." Queasy laughter. "Understood."

After this exchange, Nicky is herded over to a veritable arts and crafts buffet. He gravitates to a plastic storage bin filled with yarn, most of it rolled into tidy spheres. A bundle of knitting needles lies at the bottom. He takes a pair, chooses some yarn, and joins Denny at one of the tables. They score a spot in the shade.

It's safely removed from the child who is popping little alphabet beads into her mouth, swishing these around, and then returning them to the jar. Nicky winks at her.

As soon as they're situated, Denny subjects him to a stare that would puncture the steel hull of an aircraft carrier. "Give me Ryan's phone."

Nicky purses his lips. "Ryan? Who's that?"

"Give me Ryan's phone," his jailer says again, slowly, "while I'm still in a good mood." Denny cracks the knuckles on his enormous left hand. In a more conversational tone, he adds, "It's about midnight in Seoul, isn't it? That's pretty late, but I'm authorized to make a call."

He doesn't have to explain what this means. There's only one phone call you could ever use as a threat when dealing with Apollo.

"Jaehwan, yeah?" By now, Denny's cracked all the knuckles on his right hand as well. "Heard he's partial to his beauty sleep. Busy serving his homeland and all that. I'd hate to bug him after lights out, personally. Seems like a nice guy."

"Yep. Nicest guy on the planet." By this, Nicky means the planet Jupiter. Here on Earth, hot uncles like himself are forced to tell stories about Apollo's Jaehwan to scare their nieces and nephews into good behavior. And he doesn't want to be the unfortunate victim in any of those stories, so he surrenders his brother's phone. "He got a text earlier," he pipes up, helpfully.

"Noted."

"I didn't read it."

"Good for you."

"It was from your sister."

That line always works on Kazu, but Denny proves impervious. "It's not my lookout if Yeonnie wants to keep texting some guy with big, empty eyes and a nonexistent credit score. I've said my piece. In fact, I've said my piece to both of them."

"Yeah," says Nicky, resting an elbow on the table and propping his chin up with one hand. "I'm sure you have. But what if — and just hear me out, okay? What if, just for fun, you challenged Ari to a duel?"

Denny lets out a huge, honking guffaw. A little boy on the far end of their table tries to copy the sound, giggling.

"Need something?" Denny inquires.

The boy snaps his mouth shut. "Um, just some water," he sputters.

"Fair. Hydration is a priority. Too bad you can't walk over there and get the water yourself."

"I can, too."

Denny just shrugs. "Bet you can't," he replies. Then he turns back to Nicky like he's already moved on, even as the kid runs for the water fountain in a show of petulant self-reliance.

Well, well, well. Nicky is torn. Should he launch into a standing ovation? Should he make like those wimpy reporters and run while he still can? Regardless, he'll have to adjust his strategy. He's gone soft after months of only having to contend with a lightweight like Kazuhiko.

"Start knitting," says Denny. "Idle hands, etcetera." Nicky obliges. The needles flash, suffusing the patio with an industrious click-click-clicking. It makes him feel as though he's sitting with his ajumma friends in Seoul, everybody analyzing the latest rumors over projects like baby blankets and mittens. He's the youngest at every monthly meet-up, but he likes hanging out with them. Those ladies always have the best gossip. Most of it is about people Nicky's never met, but that part is trivial. Gossip is gossip.

"So, Chief. You want me to give the shorts back, too? That's where the phone was, you know. Like a two-for-one deal. And Ari did give me permission. He's my second nicest brother. He didn't want me to go naked, that's all."

"Permission for the shorts, or permission to take his phone?"

"Do the details really matter?" Nicky lights up with an idea. "Hey, you should check this. See if it's been bugged. That's something you know how to do, right? The passcode is 04—"

"040609. Date of birth for Ezra Goldsmith-Song, only biological sibling of Ari Goldsmith-Song, alias Song Eunjae, alias Ryan Kim."

Nicky nods, needles clacking. "Oooh, do you know his email password by any chance? I think he changed it on me."

"He did change it, Kim Ahnjong. Alias Nick, Nicky, or Nicholas Kim. Original stage name 'A.J.'"

"I've also gone by Nicodemus. Just once or twice. I replace the 'o' with a zero if I need to seem edgy. Sometimes I'll hit up the fan cafe under a fake account, just to stir things up a little."

"Member number 894525001, username MrsJess3Ahn. It's already in your file. Don't waste my time with irrelevant intel." Denny sets the tape recorder on the table between them. He presses play on the audio of Nicky's mini press conference and pauses every now and then to get clarification.

"Here, where you tell the reporters what happened on the evening of June 7, 2023. Let's talk about that."

Well, you see, I missed the flight back to Seoul on purpose. They had such a nice setup there, at Wanna Waffle. I always wanted to open my own cafe someday. Good coffee, some pastries, that kind of deal. My dad could help out on the weekends. And look, I've never mentioned this in any of my past interviews, but we used to have a place like that. It was a long time ago, before I was born. Dad had a cafe and it went under.

"Correct me if I'm wrong," says Denny. "You decided to impersonate Ryan in order to feed a false narrative to the media. This included dressing like Ryan and robbing him of his personal belongings."

"Isn't 'robbing' a strong word? It's more like I sourced this stuff through alternative channels. And before you get all huffy over it, I needed to do that. For authenticity."

"And this story you told them? Give me the rationale."

"Oh, I was just improving on the plot, there. Didn't it sound better than just saying I missed the flight because I don't wear a watch, left the hotel without my phone, and have no sense of direction? And my family did own a cafe, long ago. You need to toss in a grain of truth once in a while."

Denny inclines his head, neither agreeing nor disagreeing. "What happened to the cafe? Why'd it go under?"

Knitting imparts a sense of calm. The movements are

repetitive and barely require his brain anymore. Nicky catches a yarn ball before it can roll off the table, then replies, "Dad borrowed money from a lot of people. You know, just to get the place open. And he used all of our savings, right? Mom's money, too. But that wasn't enough, so he took out some loans."

He's fast. The rows multiply as he talks. "Couldn't pay all the money back in time, though. Not all those people lending money were very nice people, either. There were some... incidents."

"Incidents."

"Yeah." Nicky admires what he has so far, the makings of a potholder woven in blue. It could also be a table runner if he keeps going. He'll do it up in stripes, Apollo's official colors alternating in horizontal bands. "Some thugs showed up," he goes on. "And then there was the gunfight."

Denny takes a break from typing notes on his phone. "A gunfight."

"True story," says Nicky, without batting an eyelash.

"Debatable. You blamed it on a corporate buyout in a 2018 interview. And in 2021, you told a completely different story to the owner of a ramen place two blocks away from the Emerald Entertainment building."

"Wait, you talked to the nice ajumma? What'd she say? I can swing some Chanel if she needs a new bag."

"We've communicated," comes Denny's cryptic response. "Major inconsistencies occur between all versions of the cafe story, plus you change your dad's name every time."

Cheerfully, Nicky says, "Sometimes I tell people that I went into a coma for two years. It's more fun that way."

Denny's scowl might as well be permanent, chiseled into stone. Under the pressure of that unblinking stare, Nicky starts to feel like a scoop of ice cream melting in the sun.

"It is true that I've always wanted to open my own cafe. That's not a lie."

This admission earns him nothing more than a curt nod. See, this is why being honest just isn't any fun at all. There's so little return on investment. And as Nicky starts contemplating new twists to the classic sob story about his dad's cafe, Denny plays some more of the recording.

What do you know about her, though? Emma Han. Has she ever been in the news? Any major scandals? Is it true that her ex-boyfriend is a lawyer and the heir to a real estate fortune worth at least several million dollars? And this isn't for me, by the way. I'm asking for someone else.

Now the intensity of Denny's stare could liquefy both polar ice caps in a matter of minutes. Nicky realizes that his life has been in grave danger all along. He's been knitting peacefully while hurtling toward his own demise. He dares to take a breath. So this is what a near-death experience feels like! He's never come so close to perishing before. Whew, adrenaline rush!

"Tell me. Where's the wisdom in pretending to be Ryan, then asking reporters about Emma Han? If you wanted to throw them off the trail, you'd stay away from that subject."

"No way," says Nicky. "They'd be more suspicious if he never mentioned her."

"Mentioning her isn't the same as wringing them for information," Denny points out.

"I needed that information, though. Hazel's all over the place, you can find most of her scandals online. Not so for Emma. She's either got a clean record or the record's been wiped clean. The reporters didn't give me anything to work with, sad to say."

"That's fine," Denny replies. "I'll tell you. Emma Han is my sister. She's none of your business. Arthur Junior is an estate lawyer. Arthur Senior is also a lawyer, specializing in motor accidents. They're none of your business. And their combined net worth? Also none of your business."

A seagull swoops overhead. Nicky starts another row, fingers flying. "Interesting."

"Sure. Interesting." Denny leans forward. "Yeonnie's very interesting, and you're gonna leave her alone."

"Whoa, whoa. Hold on a second, Chief. I can't do that. As of last night, she's romantically involved with one of my brothers. Dating's a big no-no for people like us, but do you think Ari's done any of his homework? Do you think he has plans to do a full deep dive on the Internet so he can learn as much about her as possible? Do you think he has much of a plan, period? Of course not. Ari's just a big dope like that. Love him, but wow."

"Look, you don't have to tell me twice," Denny scoffs. "His eyes are 62% empty."

Nicky slaps both hands on the table. The children glare at him. "That's what I'm saying! Easiest swindle I've ever swindled. Never asks any questions. Can you blame me for trying to cover the bases, here? No offense, man, but Emma Han could be up to something. Maybe she only wants him for his looks."

"Not likely."

"The dreamy accent."

"That's subjective."

"Okay, maybe she's out for his bank account."

"Why? She has her own."

"You're missing the point. I can't just let Ari fall in love with the first American girl who thought to offer him a free waffle. Could you imagine? What kind of shoddy storytelling is that?"

Denny regards him with deep derision. "You think I wanted to let Yeonnie go traipsing off into the sunset with an apprentice dishwasher? I told her not to get attached to Ryan and his purple eyes. Did she listen? Nope."

Nicky chuckles. "He had purple eyes when you met him? How does he always forget his contacts? What a big dope."

"The dopiest," Denny concurs. So they agree on one thing, anyway.

"But here's my other concern, buddy. What if this big, bad lawyer ex-boyfriend decides he wants revenge?" Nicky mimes a stabbing motion with one of his knitting needles. "Revenge has been a theme lately. Look at Max, for example."

But Denny only snorts at this. "Arthur? No dice. His eyes are just as empty, my guy."

Nicky files this away for later. He breaks into a grin. "She's got a type, eh?"

"There's no accounting for taste." Denny crosses his arms.

"Ryan's alright, though," he adds. "Approachable. Honorary doctorate in customer service. Decent reflexes."

"Oh, yeah. My brother's a good guy, no question. Emma could do way worse. Our fans will hate her, that's definitely happening, but Ari? He'll love her 'til the end of time, man. He's just so boring like that. Gullible, too. And so chill. For example, why hasn't he ever picked a public fight with his mom? Ari avoids drama like I avoid telling the truth. It's a real character flaw. And I'm allowed to say this," Nicky concludes, "because that's my son we're talking about."

"He can't be both your brother and your son. Sit down."

"He's both!" Nicky contends. "And here's the bottom line: the only person scamming him is me." He pulls Ari's sunglasses out of his shirt pocket and puts them on. They're prescription, so the world becomes a dizzying blur. But the sun has grown stronger, climbing into a sky as blue as blue has ever been, and he can't be squinting at Denny Han if he wants to be taken seriously. "I've got a monopoly on that situation. Same for all my other brothers. Are we clear?"

Denny studies him, an apex predator evaluating the potential of its next meal. Is this one worth the trouble? It's a harrowing time, a sequel to Nicky's earlier brush with mortality. He ties off a potholder and starts on the next. Knitting in the face of danger! Experiment!

At last, Denny says, "I'll let it slide this time."

"I knew you'd see it my way, Chief."

"It's just too bad the reporters keep infiltrating HQ, but I guess you can't do anything about that."

The needles stop clicking. "What? Of course I can."

"Bet you can't." Denny shakes his head, then gets up to collect more yarn. He fills a paper sack with enough supplies to keep a knitting circle occupied for days. And on the bench, Nicky turns to his nearest neighbor, a little girl in a neon green swimsuit.

"Did you catch that, noona? He thinks I can't confuse a bunch of reporters. You ever heard anything so wrong in your life?" Nicky chuckles to himself. "Oh, man. Just wait and see."

In this compilation, we find some pieces that are enduring favorites among Sunshines everywhere. Half the clips feature Namgyu spiking volleyballs, throwing a javelin, and blithely sinking baskets from beyond the three-point line. Ari scores a tiebreaker goal — the happiest of accidents — before we get nine seconds of Jesse running for his life down a dark hall. This segues into some snippets from a Japanese variety show: Kazu shooting a flawless bullseye, three times in a row. Resplendent in hakama, he stands against a backdrop of glittering snow. His fans were dead on arrival.

At this point, the video jumps to footage of Apollo on stage in Kuala Lumpur. The jumbotron reads *APOLLO WORLD TOUR 2022: SOLAR FLARE.* All nine of the boys come out for an encore, no choreography, just incomprehensible levels of energy and a surprise appearance from Nicky. Benched due to an injury for most of their tour stops in Asia, he shows off his ankle wrap. The audience is ecstatic. Midway through the song, Sunny makes a surprise appearance as well. He's got a bow and a quiver of arrows fletched with electric blue feathers.

Fans will tell you that Sunny is often carrying this weapon. Sometimes it's an oversized plush lyre. These are symbolic of Apollo's namesake, the Greek god of the sun. Sunny's wreaked havoc with both props in the past, but the bow was a toy and the lyre stuffed with cotton batting. This time, the bow is not a toy. It turns out to be an actual high-performance carbon fiber longbow, lightweight and strong, six feet tall.

Sunny positions himself behind the members. He strikes a pose, painted eyes sparkling. Shrieks of mingled shock and disbelief tear through the arena as the mascot chooses Jaehwan for his target.

The arrow goes wide, skittering harmlessly off the stage. We see Kei rushing to his leader, Ari right behind him, while Max is demanding to know how their worst flipping enemy got his hands on a real bow. Namgyu misses the whole thing, lost in the music and his insane ad libs.

He bursts into tears when he realizes what happened. We can't find Jesse because he bolted behind Jungwoo and is clinging to him in full barnacle mode. As for Jaehwan, he's hopped down to comfort a woman in the front row. She emitted such a bloodcurdling scream at the prospect of seeing her bias reduced to a pincushion.

Jaehwan passes his mic to a member of the security team. He takes the woman's hands in his. "Did that scare you?" he asks, in a soothing tone that doesn't match the homicidal glint in his eyes. "Were you worried about me?"

Rendered speechless, she can only nod yes. Countless primary sources confirm that this is a normal response when interacting with Jaehwan in person. His beauty overloads the senses, inducing paralysis. Sunshines will tell you that it feels like a divine visitation, but it might be wise to consider adaptations found in nature. Like tiger stripes and false eyes, glowing lures and velociraptor frills, Jaehwan's beguiling face has the power to hypnotize and distract.

"I'm so sorry that he upset you. Sunny was just playing a game. Isn't that right, Nicky? He was playing a game too, giving Sunny a real bow."

"That's right," Nicky wheezes, nearly prostrate with mirth. "But wasn't it so funny?"

Still holding the woman's hands, Jaehwan gives her an angelic smile. "Should I make him pay?"

"S-Sunny? Or Nicky?"

The smile evolves into something altogether unworldly. "For you," says Jaehwan, "both."

This lady needs a fainting couch. She can only gaze at Jaehwan, enraptured. She's living her best life, swept away to a world of enchantment. No spell lasts forever, though. "Oppa-yah!" someone yells from a few rows back. "Just don't touch Nicky's face!"

"Don't go for his ankles either!"

"Don't touch Nicky at all! Innocent until proven guilty! FREE MY MAN." These remarks are translated by audience members into a variety of languages.

Laughter ensues. Ari asks one of the bodyguards if he can see the arrow. He crouches down to take it. "It's plastic," he informs everyone. And indeed, the arrow is tipped with a massive silver heart, cartoonish in design. This revelation has the whole arena sighing in relief. But Kei snatches it from him, studies the heart-shaped arrowhead, and exclaims that it would still hurt if it actually hit you.

"Hear me out, though," says Nicky. "Just listen, Keiichi. Nine times out of ten, Sunny will miss. Trust me, I calculated the odds. And that arrow wouldn't draw blood or anything. See? It's all floppy."

Garbled cursing from Max; a wail from Jesse. Kei waves the arrow at his brother. "That's the limit, hyung? It's fine as long as no one's bleeding out on stage?" Quite possibly developing a tic in his left eye, Kei turns to the audience next. "I hate it here," he announces in English.

This is when the stage crew decides that it's time to resume the encore. The music surges back on, and a tearful Namgyu drops right into the chorus without missing a beat. The members gather in twos and threes, arms around each other, Jaehwan in the center with his arm clamped around Nicky like a vise. The concert goers swiftly forget, caught up in the song, the feelings, the lifelong memories being made.

And yet, there's more. Someone else's recording has been spliced into the video now. It provides us with an alternate view of Sunny shooting the arrow at Jaehwan. This phone belongs to a veteran Sunshine, and she swings the camera in Kazu's direction at the moment of crisis, hustling to capture a reaction.

Well, maybe she did that just to look at him, too. Standing motionless on stage left, he's hiked up the sleeves on his pale blue concert tee, treating everyone to a gun show well worth the price of admission. Sweat glistens along that famous jawline and the legendary cheekbones. And as we're watching him, Kazu's gaze goes from Sunny to Jaehwan, then to the quiver of arrows lying forgotten at the mascot's feet. The longbow is there too, similarly forgotten.

While Sunny mugs for the cameras, facing stage right, Kazu stalks over to the longbow. He bends down to pick it up. Testing the heft of it in one hand, he collects an arrow with the other. Kazu nocks it on the bowstring. He takes aim, swiveling so that Sunny's giant, oblivious head is in his sights. Muscles strain. The string pulls taut.

And then Kazu lets the arrow fly.

Meet the Parents

Kazu

A POLLO'S NEW HIDEOUT IS a sprawling suburban residence with five bedrooms and a pool out back. Sorry, their new safehouse. Denny's terminology. Kazu keeps forgetting.

It's a quiet neighborhood, laid out in a pattern of green lawns and blocky, ranch-style houses just like theirs. Cars back out of the driveways every morning and come rolling up every evening, like clockwork. No one on this street has noticed that eight members of a K-pop group have moved in next door.

Denny's handiwork, Kazu assumes. His aunt employs several individuals with similar skill sets. She's drawn to people who are efficient, proactive, competent. How she ended up with Uncle Ren is an enduring mystery and one of the family's favorite jokes, but the point is that Denny's personality is familiar to him, and therefore comforting.

He'd been the first to support Ari's nomination of Denny Han as their unofficial manager, at least for the duration of Apollo's extended stay in Los Angeles. Really, what an inspired idea. The kid went out into the world and came back with something to show for it. That something makes Kazu's job easier, which is even better. It's just a shame that it's temporary.

God, he's tired of serving as Apollo's supreme leader. How did Hwannie fill this role for so long? Look at him on the screen, eating a late dinner, having made it all the way to his enlistment date without losing his mind. Kazu would've gone running for the hills if they'd tasked him with being in charge at such a young age.

"I'm telling you," Jaehwan says now, stabbing his chopsticks at them, "that he'll get caught within twenty-four hours if you ever let him out with her in public. But if we lock Nicky in his room without WiFi or a phone, it might get us an extra two days."

Nicky plunks his coffee mug down on the table, scandalized by this accurate observation. "Hey, now. I haven't caused any trouble for like, forty-eight hours. And I was so chill the whole time this stuff was happening. Can you imagine everything I could've done while no one was paying attention to me? But I didn't do even half of those things—"

Jaehwan's gaze sharpens. He picks up his phone, swipes a few times, then clears his throat. "Leader-nim," he reads aloud, "Nicky-hyung told a bunch of people that Ari-hyung got stranded at LAX and needs money to get back to Seoul. He's got a donation jar and a crowdfunding page. This is ridiculous, he's going to get himself arrested!"

Yikes, Kazu thinks to himself. Hwannie's reading from the folder with all the screenshots. This record of Nicky's transgressions is crammed so full that it's got to be taking up most of the phone's internal memory.

"Keiichi has too much time on his hands," the defendant argues back. "You know how the Chief's always like, 'Kim Ahnjong, idle hands do the devil's work, knit me another set of pot holders by tonight at 2100 hours'? Same principle, okay, except that His Royal Highness gets bored and tattles on me for personal entertainment. Imagine if he worked on a cure for cancer instead."

"Hyung!!!!!" Jaehwan continues, in higher, whinier tones. "Hyung PLEASE, Nicky almost got me trapped in a trash compactor, he's *demented*, I could've died so young, I could've been a showbiz tragedy!!!!"

"The machine wasn't even plugged in!"

Jaehwan doesn't bother to respond to this assertion. "Aww man, Jaehwan-hyung... is it true that Ari left so he could find his real family? Because I never knew he was kidnapped as a baby! I'd never know if Nicky-hyung didn't tell me just now. Did Leila really steal him right out of the hospital because he was a pretty baby and hers was ugly? I didn't even think she could be meaner... Jaehwan-hyung, I'm just so sad right now..."

"Haha! That was me!" Namgyu starts laughing around a mouthful of waffles. "You got me so good, Nicky. Aww, you're just the funniest!"

"And my story was better, right? Tell them, Gyu. Tell them I came up with something way better than a K-pop idol missing his flight and pretending to have amnesia. That's such a tired plot line. The writer should've consulted me first."

"You know what I'm tired of? Getting all these texts and emails about Nicky did this and Nicky did that, Nicky almost got me killed again, Nicky thought it would be funny to pay somebody to dress like Ari and walk around an airport in... let's see, what did Manager Doyoung send me..." Jaehwan flicks through some more screenshots. "Here it is. Mykonos. 'Jaehwan, we think Ari might be in Greece. Do you know why he'd go there?'"

Kazu sits up. "What? When the hell did that happen?"

"But listen," says Nicky. "Doyoung-hyung was a loser. I'm glad he finally quit. I've been working on that forever and I just really can't describe how great it feels to see a project turn out so well." He drains the rest of his coffee. "And where's my thank you card, anyway? Because of me, Emerald wasted even more time looking for Ari. I bet I got him at least an extra six hours. I'm expecting him to name the first kid Nicholas and the second kid Nicole. Like, I hope he realizes how much I contributed."

"You contributed?" Jaehwan's stare feels like a laser boring into Kazu's brain even though he isn't the primary target right now. "So you admit that you did shit you weren't supposed to be doing? You're owning up to the fact that you did the complete ass-backwards opposite when I told you to stay in your room and sit on your hands until we found Ari—"

"Hear me out, though! Technically I did sit on my hands,

since I made most of the calls with my phone on speaker, so I wasn't using my hands—"

Namgyu claps. "Haha! Hyung, you never care if you might die soon! Wow, you're the bravest."

"Ari will be fine," says Kazu, realizing he should change the subject before Jaehwan leaps through the screen to slaughter everyone in sight. "He hasn't even left the house except for meetings. No one's seen him with Jiyeon, and even if they did, she's got a good reason to be hanging around. Her brother's with us every day. We could explain that easily enough."

"The only thing that'll save Ari is going back to Seoul. There's less chance of getting caught when they're not even in the same country anymore."

"Unless someone leaks their text messages," Nicky puts in helpfully. Kazu pelts him with a crumpled napkin. "What? I didn't say it would be me! That was just some brainstorming!"

Meanwhile, Namgyu is stricken. "Aww, but they won't get to be together again for months! I forgot that would happen. It's awful! Why can't Ari just stay here? He's going to be so sad when it's time to leave!"

"He'd be sadder if the fans found out about Jiyeon," Jaehwan points out. "And we all know why. We've seen it before."

These kids have some kind of timing. Why so much scandal in one summer? Can't they give Kazu a break?

"Personally," says Nicky, claiming another waffle from the stack, "I think it's hilarious he kept all of Jungwoo's girls a secret but won't be able to manage it for himself. I'm with Mother

Dearest on that one. Doesn't anyone else think that's so funny?"

Kazu takes up a random fork. He skewers a piece of Nicky's waffle and drags it through a sticky, sugary puddle of maple syrup before popping the bite into his mouth. "Regardless, we can't let Ari mess this up. We'll lose the free food."

Yeah, Ari's probably in for a hell of a time. The whole group might suffer along with him. He's still Kazu's favorite kid right now, though. He could've picked any random family to adopt him, but he picked these nice people who make waffles. And the waffles are incredible as they are, but everybody knows that a meal tastes twice as good when it's free.

"Free food? You've been paying for that, Zu."

"Ooooh, thanks Dad!"

Kazu lowers his fork. "What?"

"International Bank of Kazuhiko!"

"Denny sends me the grocery bills," says Jaehwan, "and then I pay them."

"His money is blood and his blood is money!"

"With my credit card?"

Jaehwan's eyes flash. "Yes. Did you have something to say about it?"

Yikes. "Not really."

"That's what I figured." Jaehwan starts gathering up his dinner dishes, putting everything into a neat pile. He carries them off-screen to wash up. Kazu helps himself to the last waffle during this intermission. Then he makes sure Nicky cleans his plate, too. By god, Kazu paid for this!

"It'll be hard for him," says Jaehwan, when he returns to the video call, "but I don't see how Ari has a choice. We've agreed to finish out remaining obligations to Emerald. That includes his unit with Jungwoo and Max, since that was already lined up before he ran away, and then there's stuff on the schedule until at least September. Staying here isn't an option."

"I think he understands that. He's never said a word about not coming with us in July."

"Fine, but I won't have him moping around for the next few months. He needs to remember that this is his job. They decided to give this a shot together, and that's fine, but they have to deal with what that means. Won't be the last time he has to say goodbye to her."

Nicky points his fork at Jaehwan. "See, now how can you say that without feeling bad? I bet even Sunny would feel bad and there's nobody inside that costume except the devil."

Kazu does feel bad. He makes himself get up, wondering if there's any iced coffee left in the fridge. Oh, and some condensed milk. He'll dump a whole can in there. It would be soothing. He admires Jaehwan for being able to look even the harshest truths directly in the eye, but sometimes it's a bit much.

The house's interior is dim and cool, brimming with a delightful silence that tells him most of the younger members are still asleep. Most of them, but not Kei, who happens to be in the kitchen when Kazu comes in. He takes one look at Kazu and forgets all about the glass of orange juice he just poured for himself.

"What is wrong with you? Put a shirt on!"

"Sorry, are you my dad now?"

"Why have a closet like a Vuitton flagship store," hisses Kei, "when you walk around half naked most of the time?"

"Comfort," Kazu hisses back, "is more important than clothes."

Kei lobs an apple at him. Kazu retaliates by seizing his younger brother in a headlock. They call a ceasefire when they hear voices in the living room. The two in the kitchen creep closer, angling for a better view. Denny is with his sister, newly arrived, sunglasses on her face. In sandals, she's still taller than all the women in Kazu's family. Her hair falls down her back in a long braid.

Kazu ditches Kei and strides toward them. Ari's girl. Jaehwan wanted to talk to her anyway, so this is perfect. "Morning!" he calls out, proud of himself for remembering Hwannie's agenda. See? He remembers things. He remembers things regularly!

Denny crosses his arms. "It's the one from the Tokyo crime dynasty."

"I'm pretty sure his family runs hotels," says Jiyeon.

"That's what I said. Crime dynasty."

Kazu shrugs. Auntie Haru probably wouldn't mind that kind of rumor, and his uncle would just think it was hilarious. "Close enough."

Jiyeon turns to him with an apologetic smile. Car keys are looped around her thumb and she's got a cardboard drink carrier in her other hand. Kazu rejoices inwardly. Maybe there's a treat in there for him.

"I think the big, frothy one is yours. Looks like it's more whipped cream than anything else."

Yes! It's like she just brought him the Holy Grail. What a keeper. Ari remains his favorite kid, potentially from now until the end of time.

"How'd you know to bring coffee?"

"Oh, Denny asked me to stop on my way here."

Kazu eyes the other cups in the carrier. Although Denny never once asked for anyone's preferences, the drinks are exactly right. Plain black coffee for Namgyu, because he's a freak. A massive Americano for Nicky. And there's a latte, something complicated with a billion abbreviations scrawled on the side, as if the drink has spiraled into an identity crisis. Jungwoo's, then. Even his coffee order is existential.

"I was told Apollo has a press conference this afternoon," Jiyeon says. "The management thinks you might not be caffeinated enough for it."

Denny takes the car keys from his sister. "They'll be asleep by lunchtime at the rate they're going. The older ones were out on the street at 5am. They think they're some kind of three-man Olympic cross country team. And the one who calls himself Orpheus was out by the pool, scribbling in his notebook before the sun was even up."

"Orpheus...?"

"It's the name Jungwoo uses for producer credits," Kazu explains. "5am is his songwriting power hour. He's got all these rituals."

"Orpheus. Hmm."

"I don't care what he wants to do as long as he stays awake for the whole press conference." Denny catches sight of Kei lurking in the kitchen. "None for you, Moriyama. I know you've only been up since 9:30. You can hack it."

Kei comes marching over. He pulls off a flawless salute, his form absolutely unimpeachable. Someone's been studying all the Jaehwan fan-cams from that latest army event. "Captain! Yes, Captain! You know better than I do, Captain!"

"At ease, soldier," Denny barks back. "Come on. You can help me get the supplies out of the car. Yeonnie brought all her hair and makeup stuff since you guys had to leave most of yours behind."

Kazu insists on carrying the drinks for Jiyeon while Kei scampers after Denny like a puppy. "Got a minute?"

"Uh-huh. I think Eunjae overslept."

"Talking to someone on the phone all night. Wonder who it could be?"

She laughs. "I hope it was me."

They make a quick detour so Kazu can drop off the weird latte. He leaves it by the door and knocks twice. Jungwoo might be in there meditating, or communing with the ghosts of past heartbreaks, or whatever it is that he does to get the songs written. There's a process. It's complicated.

Delivery made, Kazu guides Jiyeon through the kitchen and out the back door, where Nicky is once again on the defense.

Jaehwan seems to be reciting a list of all the times that their resident choreographer has blurted out spoilers during his livestreams. Both look up in surprise when Kazu walks up with Jiyeon in tow.

"She brought more coffee," he announces, setting the carrier on the table, "and I brought her. Might as well do it now, right?"

"Nice, Zu. Now is perfect." Jaehwan's eyes crinkle up as he smiles at Jiyeon from the other side of the screen. It's not the murder smile, not by a long shot. This is the smile that sells out arenas. It's a thing of irresistible charm and mesmerizing power. "If you have some time," Jaehwan adds. "We won't borrow you for too long, I promise."

"Oh, sure." She smiles back at him. "Jaehwan, right? It's nice to meet you. I've missed all the other times you've been on a call with them." She bows, a formal greeting. "Eunjae says you're his mom."

"I am." Jaehwan bows to her as well. Nicky and Kazu do the same. "We just wanted to thank you. For taking care of Ari, and for offering him a home. You and your family have done so much for us."

Nicky whisks out a chair for Jiyeon, who sits down just as Namgyu comes tearing out of the pool, splashing water everywhere. "Aww, are we all bowing to each other? Why didn't you tell me?" Then he has to ask Jiyeon if she's had breakfast, how she could be so pretty again when she was so pretty yesterday, and why she doesn't have her own coffee. Would she like to have his coffee? Sensing that this could go on forever, Nicky gently escorts Namgyu toward the pool, then shoves him in. "Haha!" they hear, when he floats back to the surface. "I did want to keep swimming! Thanks, Nicky!"

"Alright, let's talk business," says Jaehwan. "Eternal gratitude aside, this is a friendly reminder that there will be no returns or exchanges. All sales are final. And as much as I'd love to off-load more than one kid at a time, this can't be combined with other offers. Do you accept the terms?"

Bemused, Jiyeon replies, "I accept."

"Great. So, Jungwoo's always done the laundry for both of them, but Ari knows how to do it too. I can vouch for that. And you already know he can wash dishes for hours. No allergies. Forgets his glasses in random places, but I fixed that long ago by making sure he has about twenty different pairs. You might want to do the same."

"Got it."

"We're going for transparency here. So let's see, pros and cons... oh, Ari plays piano almost as well as Kazu."

"My dad and grandma both play professionally," Kazu explains to Jiyeon. "It's not like I could've escaped it."

She nods. "I heard he can sing a little, too." This makes Jaehwan laugh.

"Ari's the best at packing a suitcase!" Namgyu volunteers from the water. "Rolls everything up! Those cubes you put your stuff in! Everything! Aww, it's adorable. He's so smart, I love Ari."

"He collects cameras," says Kazu. "That's good, right? It could be worse. Nicky collects pots and pans. He doesn't even have a kitchen."

"I don't collect the pots and pans. I treasure them."

"People cry on Eunjae a lot," Jiyeon brings up, resulting in nods of universal agreement from his brothers. "What's going on there?"

Kazu sighs. "You almost can't take him anywhere."

"We've never figured out why this happens. There's just something about him, I guess."

Nicky cradles his paper coffee cup in both hands and says, "The crying thing isn't a problem. Sure, you have to watch strangers weep on your boyfriend's shoulder, but think of all the gossip you can get out of it. They tell Ari all kinds of stuff. Breakups, divorces, crimes they committed, how much money they're keeping under the mattress. Focus on the possibilities, ajumma."

Jiyeon blinks at him. "Aren't you older than me?"

"That depends. On my birth certificate, which we lost in the fire—"

"A-ha!" Jaehwan exclaims. "Ari can cook five different things."

Kazu frowns. "Hey, how's that supposed to sell? Five things. That's not a lot."

"I have to be honest! Look, the sooner we get them all married off, the sooner we can retire. Especially me. You're already halfway retired because you're useless. Nice to look at, Zu, but useless."

"Just think," Nicky murmurs to Jiyeon. "This could be your future. You know? Monogamy. Oooh, and Ari told me that your first kid will be Nicholas and the second one will be Nicole. I want you to know that I'm honored." Jiyeon covers her face with both hands, laughing.

"Hwannie, I'm just saying that you could spin it a little better. My Uncle Masu, you know, he's in sales. And he'd be like, 'Ari has mastered the art of five essential entrées' or something. See? Doesn't that sound better?"

"First off, your uncle is demonic. He could sell someone their own liver, and on a subscription model. That's not normal. Second, I have to be up front about the merchandise. What do you want me to do, tell her Ari's a trained chef? Then what?"

"Ya! Being honest is one thing, but selling the kid short is another. I'm pretty sure he can make scrambled eggs. That's six things!"

"Fine, he can cook six things. There are six very basic dishes on the menu, Jiyeon."

Namgyu paddles over again. "Hyung! We gotta tell her about the *Trickster* MV! Haha, I thought of that five minutes ago and forgot it so fast."

Nicky trails off in the middle of suggesting names for a potential third child. Jaehwan and Kazu both grimace at the same time. Their reactions intrigue Jiyeon. "*Trickster*? I don't think I've seen that one yet."

"Basically, ajumma, Ari was on screen with Hazel for ten seconds and it broke the Internet."

"Jiyeon-ah! Don't read the comments, okay? Haha!"

"But hear me out. What if we all read the comments right now? Together."

Kazu takes another sip of cold, delicious, sugary coffee goodness. "Nothing happened there, no matter what people said online. He was only in the water with Hazel for fifteen minutes."

"Twenty," amends Jaehwan. "They couldn't do it in one take because Ari kept apologizing to her. Never mind all the morons on set who were interrupting to give him advice. Bunch of backseat drivers. Like any of you know shit."

"Hey, I know shit."

"Do you?"

Nicky's eyebrows suddenly become quite expressive. "Kazu looks like he knows shit, so that counts for a lot."

"What the hell is that supposed to mean?"

"In the water...?" Jiyeon frowns, trying to puzzle out what they're saying. "What was he apologizing for? And Hazel is...?"

"An actress. She was in the video with us." Nicky can't finish the sentence without giggling madly. "Max's girlfriend," he manages to croak. Within seconds, Jiyeon is surrounded by men who can't stop laughing. They're all doubled over, at risk of falling out of their chairs. Namgyu actually does slide right off the unicorn pool float. He vanishes underwater for a hot second, then comes up gasping for air, peals of laughter ringing out across the neighborhood at large.

"Hahahahaha!"

"Oh, man. Oh, I think I'm dying."

"Hazel!" Jiyeon snaps her fingers, connecting with the name at last. "Eunjae told me what happened, but it was hard to follow the story. I guess I didn't catch her name. He was laughing the whole time."

"Hahahahaha!"

Kazu's face hurts and it feels like he did a thirty minute ab workout. "Anyway," he tells Jiyeon, "if you ever watch *Trickster*, just remember that it was all acting. If it looks real, it's because Hazel is good at her job."

"And Ari's good at following directions," Nick chimes in, eyebrows becoming highly expressive again. "See, that's another good reason to keep him around."

Jiyeon jumps a little as a pair of hands comes down to cover her ears. Ari has stolen up from the house without anyone noticing, evading detection while his brothers were in hysterics over Max.

"What have you been saying to her?"

"Nothing bad!" Kazu hastens to assure him.

"We came up with, like, a million reasons not to dump you. And you already know this, my son, but I accept gratitude in cash only."

"Thank you," says Ari, with feeling. "Never speak to her again," he adds, with even more feeling.

"What!"

"But we like her!"

"Aww, I wanted to keep talking to my new sister forever..."

"I needed to thank her in person," says Jaehwan. "This is the best I can do right now, since you're over there and I'm over here."

Kazu slurps at the dregs of his iced coffee. He adds, "If it makes you feel better, Hwannie had a chat with Hazel, too."

"Oooohh, leader-nim! You've been holding out on me! What did you say? What did she say? Sharing is caring—"

Jiyeon removes Ari's hands from her ears. She tugs him forward a little, just so his arms wrap around her shoulders. Turning partway, she glances up at him and says, "You have nice parents. I accepted their terms and conditions."

"I see," he replies, smiling at her. "I think I'd better go over those too."

"They told me all about the chores you know how to do. Also, you can cook six things, pack a suitcase, and play the piano."

"No wonder you signed on for life."

"Well. You *are* really good at following directions. That's a plus."

The scene immediately implodes. Nicky leaps up so fast that his patio chair tips over backwards. Kazu crushes his empty drink cup by accident. Jaehwan is rendered speechless, for once, and Namgyu goes missing once again, his last known location marked by some air bubbles near the pool ladder.

"Ajumma, come whisper it in my ear. What kind of directions?"

Kazu rubs at his temples. "Ari-yah. This is... You need to... I mean, that's between the two of you, but..."

"What's happening to them?" Jiyeon asks Ari, perplexed. "Did I say something weird? I was just agreeing—"

"Okay," says Ari, taking her by the hand. "Time to go inside. Why are you guys even out here? It's so hot."

"Is it, my son?" Nicky calls out to him. "On a scale of one to five, how hot is it, exactly?"

"Aww, did you see that look on Ari's face? Right before he almost passed out. Haha! And I almost passed out too, whew! Jiyeon's so funny. I love her so much!"

"When he first walked up, though." Jaehwan emits a low whistle. "I didn't even know the kid had a murder smile."

Kazu didn't either. But that other smile — the one Ari held back just for Jiyeon — it's as familiar to him as Denny's ruthless efficiency, and even more comforting to see.

As Nicky jumps into the pool with Namgyu, Kazu thinks about his family. How lucky he was, to grow up believing that everybody's parents smiled at each other that way. To know with such certainty that as soon as he walked through the door, he'd be mobbed by people who loved him.

He knows it's not what Ari had, growing up. But he's glad, so glad, that he got it from Apollo. Maybe Kazu and Jaehwan didn't always make the right call, tasked as they were with keeping all these kids in line when they were just kids themselves. But Kazu feels confident that they did right by Ari, and now he can be loved by other people too.

"My god, Zu. You're thinking what I'm thinking, right?"

Kazu returns to reality. He realizes that Jaehwan is staring at him, scowling to high heaven. "That I need to go home and see my mom?" After a beat or two, he adds, "Okay, my dad too, I guess. For five seconds."

"No, but go home if you want. Hug your pretty sister for me."

"Yeah, alright," says Kazu. He leans back, propping both bare feet on the table. "I deserve that."

"Deadbeat dad," Jaehwan goes on, laughing. "The worst."

Kazu laughs with him. "Yep. Fine."

"I'm just kidding. Look at everything you've accomplished since you took over. Nobody's cracked their head open and there's only been one mutiny. You might want to tell Ari he needs to leave his bedroom door open, but at least you managed to make two of these idiots someone else's problem. That beats my track record."

Oh, man. The door. He never even thought about the door! "Thanks, Hwannie. You're a tough act to follow."

"You're right. I am."

"What were you thinking, though?"

"I'm changing my bet." Jaehwan pinches the bridge of his nose. "Did you see the way he looked at her? Even one day is too generous. Ari's getting caught the next time he steps off this property."

Transcribed from footage shot by Apollo members Kei and Jesse. A heavily edited version was incorporated into an episode of the group's long-running YouTube series, Shine Bright Apollo. *Look for Season 7, Episode #3.*

Apollo member JESSE waves to the camera. He's standing in a living room outfitted with mid-century modern furniture, and we can see a few other people in the background. NICKY and NAMGYU are seated on the long sofa, in conversation with a visiting MRS. HAN. The voices of DENNY and MR. HAN can be heard, even though they're both in the backyard.

Kei: You said you were ready.

Jesse: (*towel-drying his hair*) I am!

Kei: (*silence, presumably because he's glaring*)

Jesse: I'm ready, I'm ready. Look, I've got the video pulled up and everything.

Kei: It's almost time for dinner. We should've started earlier, and now Denny's busy. We'll be bothering him again.

Jesse: (*whines*) You need to like... do yoga or something, hyung. I can feel my skin breaking out every time I look at you, it's so stressful, like why can't you just put on a sheet mask or take a bubble bath —

Kei: HURRY UP!

[PAUSE]

Now the scene is more composed. With the towel still draped over his shoulders, JESSE addresses the audience with a megawatt grin.

Jesse: Sunshiiinnneeeessss! It's me, your favorite! We miss you so much. Do you miss us too? There's a pool here so I've been swimming every single day! It's great. I haven't gotten to swim in forever! Did you know I suffer so much? Hyungs never want to buy me a pool for my birthday, not even the ones who have money... (*stares *into the middle distance*) It's a tragedy. You feel sorry for me, right, Sunshines?

Namgyu: (*comes running over*) Awwww!!! Are we doing a live? Are Sunshines here right now? Sunshinnneeessssss!

Jesse: It's not live, hyung. We're making something. Kei's helping me, see? Keiichi-hyung, say hi to Sunshines.

Kei: (*turning the camera on himself*) Sunshines, how are you? (*formal bow; not smiling*) Have you eaten yet? It's almost time for dinner here. (*muttering*) And Nicky-hyung isn't cooking, so maybe we won't end up poisoned.

Jesse: Oh my gooosssshhhh, did you guys know Keiichi is the most dramatic? He still hasn't forgiven Nicky for making fries out of sweet potatoes instead of normal potatoes. Nobody's getting poisoned!

Namgyu: Awwww!!!

Jesse: ANYWAY. Lots of crazy things have happened to us, and now we have a new manager! He's the BEST! We LOVE him! I saw that you guys have sooooo many questions, but I can't really tell you much, he said it's classified or something—

Kei: (*harsh whispering*) The Captain didn't even agree to be our manager yet! Shut up!

Jesse: (*whispering back*) He's going to. He'll say yes if we get Ari-hyung to ask him. So you shut up and quit giving yourself more work to do. Now you'll have to edit this out!

Namgyu: Oh! Are we talking about Ari-hyung's

brother-in-law? Haha!

Jesse: (*blows raspberry at Kei*) Have fun editing, hyung!

Kei: (*more muttering*)

Jesse: So we have a new manager and we thought it would be fun if we showed him our music videos. He hasn't seen most of them. We'll record his reactions! You want to watch that, don't you? Today we're doing the MV for *Break Point*!

Namgyu: Awww man, I'm so excited! What a great idea, what a smart baby brother!

Jesse: (*preens*) Yep!!! Are you ready? Gyu, go get the Captain. It's time!

Kei: (*calling after Namgyu*) Ask him nicely! Be respectful! (*gets up*) No, I can't do this. I need to go with him and make sure he's not embarrassing—

BREAK POINT (2021)

The camera flies over a desert landscape for what seems like miles and miles. Then it descends in a slow spiral. Details emerge, half buried in the dunes: an epaulet; a jeweled cuff; the toe of a leather boot, polished to the highest shine. Why, there's a prince here! A sleeping prince, long lashes dusted with sand.

[PAUSE]

Jesse: Captain! Denny! Boss! Are you paying attention? Are you watching this? (*whines*) You said you'd watch!

Denny: (*in an apron; still holding some grill tongs*) Kim Ahnjong. When I tell you that I want a full set of coasters for every table in my restaurant by 2100 hours, I'm not joking around. Find your crochet hook or I'll find it for you.

Nicky: But hear me out, Chief. I need breaks once in a while. Work-life balance, you know? Gotta refill the creative well. (*turning to Mrs. Han*) Noona, did you know there was this one time when Jesse almost got stuck in a well—

Jesse: Because of you! (*wailing*)

Mrs. Han: (*takes Nicky's face in both hands*) Nicky, you could be a very nice boy. A very, very nice boy, yes? But why are you like this? Your mommy and daddy, they know you act this way?

Nicky: Wish I could tell you. Sadly, I've never met them. When our house burned down—

Denny: (*sets the tongs on the table with a thump*)

[PAUSE]

This is no peaceful slumber. The prince frowns, and then images flash across the screen, too fleeting and fragmented to comprehend. We catch a glimpse of the sea, a chandelier, and the trailing hem of a ballgown. One hand reaches for another, only to close on empty air. Flames leap into a sky crowded with stars.

The prince opens his piercing green eyes—

Denny: Why can't any of you have an eye color that makes sense?

Kei: Don't people have green eyes, Captain?

Denny: (*takes a deep breath, poised to discuss the basics of dominant and recessive genes and how these determine physical characteristics such as eye color*)

Jesse: (*presses play again*)

As our prince treks across the dunes, two others rise from the sand and fall into step beside him. Their knee-high boots with platform soles should be useless on this terrain. No one has any difficulty, though. K-pop is a magical, lawless place. Mathematics? Arbitrary. Physics? Optional.

The three princes trudge onward. Kazu's hair is the longest it's ever been and ever will be, shining in the sun and somehow not smacking him in the face with every dramatic gust of wind. The camera zooms in as Nicky shields his eyes from the glare, allowing us to admire the perfection of his lip gloss. All three men are equipped with sword belts, gaudy masterpieces studded with gems. But only one prince has a cape stitched with golden suns, and he's also the only one wearing a circlet on his brow. An emerald gleams from the center. I'm sure you've guessed by now that this prince... is Apollo's leader, Jaehwan.

[PAUSE]

Denny: So Jaehwan is some kind of prince.

Namgyu: Aww, he is!

Denny: And the other two are... also princes.

Jesse: Yeah, Zuzu and Nicky.

Denny: But they're not as important.

Kei: (*snorts*)

Denny: They're like... lesser princes.

Kei: (*openly laughing*)

Mrs. Han: (*comes over to pat Kei on the cheek*) I don't think I've ever heard this one laugh before. You have a nice laugh! Laugh some more, okay?

Namgyu: Awww! He's got the nicest laugh, I love him so much!

Our royal trio approaches a trickle of sand that falls from the sky. Nicky looks up and the camera pans with him, revealing that the desert isn't as vast and open as they thought. In fact, this strange place and our vagabond princes are trapped within the bounds of an hourglass the size of a world.

They look to one another, attempting to process this revelation. And then a sinkhole opens beneath their feet! The princes are devoured by an abyssal maw. The screen goes dark, and APOLLO: BREAK POINT appears in glowing, stylized letters. Now, the music video can truly begin.

[PAUSE]

Denny: That was only the intro? (*squints at the laptop screen*) This runs for almost EIGHT MINUTES? Jesus, why?

Jesse: Captain, this is art, okay? It's *cinema*.

Denny: Wrong. This is tomfoolery.

Mrs. Han: (*off-screen, in the kitchen*) Who is this Tom? What are you watching?

Denny: I'm not watching anymore, I need to get back outside. I left Dad at the grill. This can't be eight minutes of my life.

Kei: (*bows*) Understood.

Jesse: WAAAAAHHHHH CAPTAIN YOU SAID YOU'D WATCH WITH MEEEEEE

The actual music video begins with a dance segment. All nine members execute the point choreography in formation, the scene

alternating between a rain-slick street and a hall carved entirely from marble. In the street scenes, the boys wear jeans and bespoke blazers encrusted with rhinestones. At the marble palace, they're dressed as 18th century European royalty, but make it fashion. How they're able to manage dancing while weighted down with so much jewelry and gold braid is beyond our ken as mere mortals. Kei and Jungwoo split the first verse —

[PAUSE]

Denny: Moriyama. Who decides which words are randomly in English?

Kei: Jungwoo-hyung, I guess?

Denny: And how does he decide? Why say the word 'broken' in English but the rest is in Korean, what's the logic behind picking that word?

Jesse: It's not about logic, boss. It's about vibes.

Denny: Vibes.

Jesse: (*nodding*) Yep. No logic. Just vibes. Only the vibes, forever.

Denny: ....

Jaehwan, Kazu, and Nicky plummet through time and space. They land in the bustling environs of modern-day Seoul. Wandering about in a daze, they're eventually separated. Prince

Nicholas enters a market thronged with vendors, where Jesse and Namgyu have been cornered by enemies clad in ninja-inspired attire. Prince Kazuhiko takes shelter in the lobby of a hotel. Ari and Kei drop down from a chandelier to shield him from assassins.

[PAUSE]

Denny: So you're all supposed to be princes, but only one of you is important.

Jesse: That's how it is in most of our videos.

Denny: And the non-princes are... bodyguards? (*muttering to himself*) No, they're dressed in similar nonsense clothes so they must be operating as decoys as well as bodyguards... decent strategy... executed in the stupidest way possible...

Kei: I never thought about it that way... the Captain is so observant...

Namgyu: Awww, I thought it was more like hyungs are senior princes and the rest of us are still trainees. And one day, we might debut as princes!

Denny: Right. The rest of you are expendable.

Namgyu: AWWWW!

Right after another dance cut, we cover our eyes and scream as Prince Jaehwan is nearly flattened by a bus — but he's saved, at the very last moment, by a young woman in scrubs. She grabs him by the back of his princely jacket and yanks him out of the crosswalk. A nurse, she wears a hospital lanyard and a necklace with a butterfly pendant. Judging from the way time slows down when their eyes meet, this stranger is undeniably... Prince Jaehwan's one, destined true love.

They can't stare at one another for long, though. Max comes out of nowhere, tackling Jaehwan to the ground. Jungwoo seizes the nurse by the wrist and pulls her into an embrace as bullets go flying.

[PAUSE]

Kei: (*shakes head*) He wasn't supposed to hug her like that, it wasn't in the script.

Jesse: (*whispering*) Shut up! You'll have to edit that too! Oh my gosh, hyung!

Denny: Why do the enemies have terrible aim? How do you miss at practically point blank range? Incredible.

Jesse: Oh, but Captain! (*points to the nurse*) Did you know that's Ruby-noona from Athena? They're our seniors at Emerald.

Namgyu: Haha! I just realized... Jungwoo got so many girlfriends from music videos!

Jesse: Waaaahhhh, be quiet! We can't talk about that, either! Will anything be left after we edit this?

Kei: Yeah. Ten seconds total, maybe.

Jesse: (*wails*)

In the music video's most iconic dance sequence, we bear witness to the choreography that cemented Nicky's reputation as a dancer, but also as the bane of his brothers' lives on every level. The footwork is maddening. The pace is sadistic. Attempting to dance Break Point while also singing demands a pact with the devil, one which requires surrendering your soul in exchange for survival. The fact that Namgyu can still belt the chorus on a live stage without expiring is a testament to his vocal prowess. We certainly have footage of Ari having to lay down on the floor after performing this song live, and he's no slouch as a vocalist either.

[PAUSE]

Mr. Han: Look at that! These boys, so talented!

Denny: Dad. If you're in here, who's at the grill? That's an actual fire!

Mr. Han: Oh, that smart boy, Nicky—

Namgyu: Wow! Aww, man. The Captain moves so fast, I couldn't even follow him with my eyes! That's amazing!

Jesse: Skipping this... I never want to relive that choreo again, it's the worst, I hate it so much...

Kei: Do you ever think about about all the ways

Nicky-hyung's tried to kill us since we first met him? (*shudders*) Because I do...

Jesse: Stop! I said to quit stressing me out! The way these bad thoughts are clogging my pores...

Top-heavy exposition gives way to an onslaught of action sequences which the director crammed into the last ninety seconds of the video. One minute we're on the night shift at the hospital, where the heroine has hidden three handsome men in an empty supply room, and then we're somehow speeding after Kazu and Ari on a motorcycle. While Kazu weaves through bumper-to-bumper traffic, Ari rides behind him with a crossbow. He fires a bolt at their pursuers. The enemy vehicle explodes.

[PAUSE]

Denny: First of all, the one from the crime family has a higher proficiency in archery. Why give the crossbow to Ryan? Poor allocation of resources. Second, this would never work in real life. The recoil on that bow—

Kei: (*laughing*) Crime family...

Denny: And what happened to Moriyama? Wasn't he with those two at the hotel?

Jesse: Captain, you already said we were expendable, you don't have to remind Keiichi about it again. That's just rubbing salt in the wound or whatever. Hyung only looks like he has no feelings. He has them, though! I swear!

Namgyu: (*sniffles*) He was always alive in my heart. It didn't show anything bad happening to Keiichi-kun. We're just supposed to assume, but I don't have to do that if I don't want to. Ha.

Denny: ... And what about the damages? Is this coming out of the city's budget? How can you guys just destroy a whole block like this? I'm telling you that I have questions.

Kei: Don't cry about it, Gyu. It was all just pretend. Big dummy.

Namgyu: (*sniffles again*) I'm not crying... haha.............

The action scenes are interspersed with flashbacks of Jaehwan and the young nurse in all their previous lives before this one. They picnic under cherry blossoms and walk along a seashore holding hands. In the Joseon era, he presents her with a gift: a beautiful pendant wrought into the shape of a butterfly. Under another sky and in another time, the pair makes a pinkie promise to stay together forever. But in every timeline, they're torn apart by the same shadowy beings now chasing Apollo with swords. Oh, and the ninja men also have halberds. Bladed fans. A dagger made of pure crystal.

Denny: Crystal. That's what it's made of. Really?

Jesse: (*squealing*) Ohmygoshohmygosh OH MY GOSH CAPTAIN JUST WAIT. Just wait!!!! Best part of the video!!!! Aaahhhh I'm skipping straight there!!!!

Namgyu: But how is it the best part, it makes me so sad... aww, it still makes me wanna cry and it's been years...

Jesse staggers into Kazu's arms, a trickle of blood dripping down his chin. He clutches at the crystal dagger now buried between his ribs. Kazu lets out a howl of anguish, cradling the youngest member of Apollo as death comes to claim him too soon —

[PAUSE]

Denny: Jesus.

Kei: (*rolling eyes*)

Jesse: You're the worst, Keiichi-hyung. Gyu can cry for you but not for me? I was just as expendable as you were, I was super expendable—

Kei: That's not a good thing! Idiot!

Namgyu: (*small sob*) Baby brothers...

Mrs. Han: (*peeking over Denny's shoulder*) Oh, look at this kid! You're an actor, huh?

Jesse: (*back to preening*)

Mrs. Han: And Kazuhiko, look how sad he is! That part isn't acting. He loves you so much!

Jesse: (*grinning*) I'm so precious to him, right? Zuzu was so sad. He was *devastated*. Like, I bet he wouldn't do that if it was Max who got stabbed with a crystal.

Denny: Just... Christ on a crutch.

When all seems lost, the nurse's eyes flutter open. Sobbing, she crawls over the sand, wrapping her fingers around the hilt of a jeweled sword. The emeralds gleam, reflecting her tear-stained face. Step by agonized step, our heroine battles the raging winds until she's standing at the very edge of the desert, to the wall of glass that keeps them imprisoned in this hellscape. The nurse lifts her sword. She slams the hilt into the barrier again and again. Cracks form, growing wider and wider, and then the hourglass shatters.

[PAUSE]

Denny: Why didn't anybody try that from the beginning...?

Kei: Captain... please trust me. It's better if you stop asking questions. This is how I've gotten through nine years, so far.

Time flows in reverse. Jaehwan rises from the sand once again, and Jesse stumbles backward out of Kazu's arms, his mortal injury undone. The members of Apollo form a ring around their savior.

Then, everything blurs until we've returned to that cavernous hall of marble, following a woman in green taffeta as she runs into the arms of her prince. A butterfly lands on her hair. The screen darkens. A single word appears: ~fin

Jesse: (*nose in the air*) Everything made sense to me. I don't know why you guys act like it's confusing. If I didn't have trauma from dancing the choreo a hundred million times, I'd say this is my favorite video.

Kei: And you'd be the only one saying it...

Namgyu: Ha, but Ruby-noona was so good! She was so brave!

Jesse: Right? But what did you think, boss? You loved it. I know you loved it.

Denny: ....

Namgyu: He totally loved it! Just look at his face! Awwww!

Silver Medal

Jungwoo

I T'S 5:54PM. JUNGWOO HAS packed his bag and cleaned his room even though he could've procrastinated. Tomorrow morning, Denny will start ferrying them to a new hiding place because staying in one location for too long makes Apollo easier to find. Oh, hold on. Safehouse, not hiding place.

Jungwoo didn't bring much, and packing it up could've waited until after dinner, but what else is there to do? And anyway, it kept his brain busy for a while. The packing more than the cleaning, since there wasn't much to cross off on that list. He barely used anything except the bed and the desk, over the course of three days.

There's a lot less to clean up when you don't have a

roommate anymore.

Not that Ari was a messy roommate. But one is easier to clean up after than two, and there's so much less to consider when the only person occupying the space is you. Jungwoo doesn't have to check if Ari forgot his phone charger in the wall plug, or if he remembered to grab the pair of glasses he left on top of the dresser. He's got no one to look out for at present except himself.

And Jungwoo would be lying if he said that he'd never imagined such a scenario coming to pass. One day, he was going to move out of the dorms, of course. One day, Ari would naturally cede his place to someone else, someone whose name Jungwoo didn't know yet. That one great love of his life. The one he was always meant to find.

It wasn't supposed to be like this. He'd never figured it would be up to him to step aside, take the silver medal. Or maybe he's down to bronze now. That's if there's even space for Jungwoo in Ari's new life; he understands that he doesn't necessarily deserve it.

"But don't you think that's weird?" Hazel asked him once, in the flickering dark of a movie theater. They used to meet up if they were in the same city, and if the gaps in their schedules could be made to align. Always a movie in the last week of its run. Always a midweek, midday matinee or the very last showing of the night. They usually had the place to themselves, and that suited their purposes just fine.

That night, Jungwoo hadn't understood where she was coming from. Why would it be weird, for him to just keep living at the dorms and splitting a double with Ari? He saw no reason to trade the comfort of that life for anything less than a new era, the end of one epoch and the beginning of the next. Something earth-shattering, like true love. Ari was a great roommate. If the new roommate wasn't The One, why switch?

"We're fine, though," he'd told Hazel. "Emerald likes for us to stay at the dorms. It's not like we'd get kicked out. There's a security team, a night watchman, and the rest of the complex just one building over. I can walk to the studio whenever I want. I'm there a lot, so it just makes sense."

"You never think about moving out?"

"Sometimes," he'd replied with a shrug. "And if we ever felt like it, we could find an apartment like Jaehwan did."

Hazel had laughed, a sound so delicious that Jungwoo reached for her on pure impulse, kissing her until the laughter melted into a sigh. But she wouldn't let it go even after that. "You could move out into different apartments," he remembers her saying. "You'd have a place, and Ari would have a place. There's no rule saying you need to wait for marriage to stop being roommates." Then she'd turned her head, face angled toward the screen. "You could just grow up."

"You're not grown up unless you live alone? Is that what you're telling me?"

"You never listen, baby. I'm saying that you guys could live without each other if you tried. But you can't seem to imagine that happening, and it's kinda weird. Cute, I guess, but weird."

"When would we ever need to live without each other? We're

brothers."

She'd laughed again when he said this. Sometimes, Hazel would laugh and Jungwoo would want to keep the warmth of it for later, certain he could never get enough. Other times, her laugh felt more like the cold rasp of a razor against his skin. He often failed to understand what she found so funny about what he'd said.

Jungwoo isn't used to being left behind. He's lost Ari and he's lost Hazel, too. If he ever truly had Hazel. He has to admit that this was never something he could say for sure. Scrolling through their chat log yields a wealth of excuses and noncommittal responses from both sides. The silence that followed their last rip-roaring fight over the phone was not the silence of being too busy or too tired to reach out. When she confirmed the so-called dating news with Max, it was the most concrete statement either of them had ever made about their relationship.

That chat log is Jungwoo's only souvenir from his time with her. Soon, he'll delete that too. He's cultivated a habit of never saving anything that could be incriminating later, so there aren't any ticket stubs or receipts, and definitely no photos.

For obvious reasons, the tabloids have no recent photos of Max and Hazel either, not together. The media's been forced to pair those scintillating headlines with solo shots: Max, scowling in an ad for a jewelry brand, and Hazel on the red carpet at a premiere, decked out in spike heels and a backless dress. She's cut her hair to reprise a role. The strands just barely graze her shoulders as she blows a kiss to someone off-camera.

They're beautiful, taken individually. Side by side, they're absolute overkill. It's everything an audience loves to devour.

He's tried to give himself plenty of time and as many blank notebook pages as necessary, just to see if anything can be mined from his complex emotions — words to be crafted into lyrics, or perhaps a melody to expand into the beginnings of a song. But the muse remains unresponsive, huddled in the depths of Jungwoo's skull. A cornered beast licking its wounds.

He drums his pen on the windowsill. Jungwoo chose this room for the view of the backyard with its sparkling pool, visible through a scrim of overgrown flowers. He has no idea what the flowers are, but they've gone bursting out of their bounds here, so tall that their white petals brush against the panes.

You could just grow up. Is this what Hazel meant? Growing up and growing away from each other?

Outside, Jesse and Nicky play some bizarre cross between badminton and volleyball. Kazu floats in the pool, acting as the most lackadaisical referee imaginable. And on the grass, Ari and the new girlfriend have been deep in discussion for the past half hour. They don't notice the sun going down, the light transmuted from gold to silver.

Jungwoo studies the girl and doesn't even bother striving for dispassionate objectivity. His curiosity is insatiable. What is Jiyeon like? Why is she the one to finally turn Ari's head after so many long years of romantic indifference? Will Ari ever tell him about her?

She stayed behind the other day, while Denny and Mr. Han drove Apollo to the press conference in two black vans. Having forgotten to grab his sunglasses, Jungwoo was the last out of the house and the only one to catch Ari kissing Jiyeon goodbye on the way out the door.

It was nothing epic, just the quickest kiss, but full on the mouth and with his hand curved against her cheek, her fingers briefly twined around his wrist. No embarrassment, no fanfare. No slow motion zoom paired with a ballad, like you'd get in a drama episode. And yet, somehow, sweeter than anything Jungwoo had ever seen. He shrank back into the hallway and lingered there in a state of shock for far too long. Long enough that Denny started honking the horn with increasing vehemence.

Who is this girl, and what has she done to Jungwoo's best friend? How does Ari know how to kiss someone like that? How did he learn it in less than two weeks?

Jungwoo twirls the pen, listless, watching the sunset that everyone else is ignoring because they're busy enjoying life. And then he sees Ari get up, holding out his hand to help Jiyeon to her feet. She walks with him to the back door. *Best to stay right here,* he thinks, as they exit his line of sight. If he just stays in his room, Jungwoo can't accidentally witness another tender moment that will have him questioning the meaning of his entire existence.

Ari turns back, though. Kazu calls out to him and he crosses to the pool alone, unhurried, laughing at whatever is being said. Which means the girl might not be leaving yet. She's in the house, and Jungwoo could catch her alone for a moment, maybe. This is something he's been putting off, but it might be the right time. He marshals his courage and unzips the bag he just finished packing.

When he finds what he's looking for, he goes in search of Jiyeon.

He runs through a mental roll call as he hurries down the hallway. Who's here? Which brothers might wander onto the scene? Because Jungwoo can't have that. His nerves are about to fail him as it is.

Outside, in the backyard: Kazu, Jess, Nicky, Ari. Expressing appreciation for the gorgeous weather they've had so far. Talking about petitioning Denny for a fire pit. ("I don't think he'd trust us with a real fire," laments Jesse.)

Inside, holed up in the back bedroom for another day in a row: Max. He comes out three times daily to sit through meals in a simmering rage, making poor eye contact and even poorer conversation.

Out running errands with Denny: Namgyu, happy to go with anybody, anywhere. And Kei, disguised as a normal boy with terrible fashion sense, the giddiest he's ever been in public. Keiichi loves structure like Kazu loves money. Jungwoo isn't sure when they'll be back, but at least they're not in the house.

So, the coast is clear. And Jiyeon is easy to track down, spotted through the living room blinds as she fetches something from her car. He puts his hand on the knob, then aborts the mission when he sees her walking back up the driveway, headed straight for him.

Jungwoo bolts around the corner. He smacks into Namgyu and Kei, already back from running errands. How? Frantic, he shoves them both into the nearest room, which houses the washer and dryer and smells pleasantly of fabric softener.

In a noisy whisper, Namgyu asks, "Why are we hiding in the laundry room?"

In an even noisier whisper, Kei replies, "Because hyung's spying on Ari's girlfriend. You're such a big dummy sometimes, Gyu."

Jungwoo keeps an eye out for Jiyeon. "I'm not spying on her! And how'd you finish errands so fast? You're not supposed to be here."

"Aww, are you sure you're not spying on her? I would be spying on her if I were you."

"Of course we're done with errands," sniffs Kei. "The Captain never wastes time."

"Like, if my best friend ditched me for his one true love," Namgyu continues babbling at Jungwoo, "and I had betrayed him so he was never talking to me again, but I wanted to know all about this girl he loves because I care about him so much, he's my best friend, then I would be doing the exact same thing you're doing right now!" He takes a breath, finally. "Ha!"

"Hey, Ari's talked to me," falters Jungwoo. "He's definitely talked to me since... since then." They're on speaking terms. It's just that Jungwoo hasn't been initiating any conversations. Or maybe it would be better to say that he's been dodging any possibility of having a conversation. He stares at the tiled floor. "You think she's his one true love? Really?"

His brothers shrug in unison. "She could be," says Kei. "Who knows? It hasn't even been a month yet."

"Right! He's happy with her and she's happy with

him. That's what matters! Keiichi's so smart. You're the best, Keiichi-kun."

"Let go of me—"

"Keiichi-kuuuuuuunnn!"

Jungwoo breathes in the clean laundry smell, trying to calm down. Doing laundry has always been his chore. He wonders if Ari will move out of their double and go live on his own, just like the scenario Hazel described. Then he remembers that Apollo left Emerald Entertainment, so none of them have to live in the dorms anymore. It's not even an option. They're free. Untethered, with so many different paths to choose from. And what none of his brothers has said yet, even if they might be thinking it, is that they don't need to pick the same path. They don't even need to pick the same direction.

Where does Apollo go, from here?

Will Ari even come back to Seoul?

"You should just talk to him," Kei says now. "Hyung isn't mad at you anymore."

Namgyu nods in agreement. "You were just scared. And now you feel kinda jealous, but that's okay. It makes sense."

Jungwoo wasn't thinking of it as jealousy, but he can admit that his brothers are right. He's jealous that this happened for Ari first and not for him. Ari, who wasn't even looking for a love story. It's hard to accept the feeling, to name it, because it only paints him as something worse than what he already was.

He's caught between hysterical weeping and hysterical laughter. Sometimes it's rough living with so many people who know you too well. So little about yourself can remain opaque.

"I don't want to get in the way. Ari's doing great right now and I just feel horrible. I don't think I've stopped feeling horrible since the night I told Emerald how to find him. And now he has… everything that I wanted for myself. So it's like a punishment. Right? I'm being punished."

"Park Jungwoo," Namgyu replies, seizing Jungwoo's nose and pinching it. Hard. His smile is brilliant and bulletproof, a banner flown high from a fortress of impenetrable good cheer. "You're being punished? That's so silly. It's not always about you, okay? Haha! Come on."

Kei jams both hands into his pockets. He seldom deigns to wear anything so pedestrian as a hoodie and seems to be testing out how the other half lives. "I don't see what you did wrong. You had to tell the company where he was. It's not like he could've just stayed there forever, pretending to be somebody he's not. Even if you never betrayed him—"

"Why do you guys keep using the word *betrayed*—"

"Even if you never betrayed him," Kei repeats, talking over Jungwoo, "he'd still have to deal with the consequences eventually. You just made it happen faster. And everybody needed to hear what was on that contract. Who knows how long Ari-hyung would've put it off if you hadn't shown up to ruin everything for him? I think you made the right choice."

"You really think I ruined everything…?"

"Maybe he could've done it in a nicer way, though," suggests Namgyu, mouth turned down in distress. "A way that didn't make anybody cry. Ask me how to do it next time you betray someone, then I can try to think of ideas. Got it, Jungwoo? Teacher Hong is here for you. Ha!"

"A nice betrayal? Seriously?" Kei rolls his eyes again, but with a mix of fondness and consternation. "Anyway, hyung, if you want to talk to Ari's secret girlfriend that he isn't supposed to have, just go do it. Big dummy." He kicks at the laundry room door so that it swings outward into the hall. "Why are you all the biggest dummies? How are you older than I am?"

Namgyu sticks his head out. "Jiyeon-ah! Come here really fast!" he hollers in Korean.

"That's the Captain's sister," scolds Kei. "Be respectful."

"Oh!" A second attempt is made. "Cherished and beautiful Jiyeon! Could you please spare a moment of your time?"

"I said be respectful, not embarrassing! Weirdo!"

Jiyeon retraces her steps, looking justifiably confused. Namgyu ushers her into the laundry room with the formality of a butler, copied from something he saw on TV. Then he scurries off with Kei, the pair of them making such a rapid exit that there should've been a cloud of smoke in their wake.

Jungwoo is now standing in a cramped space with someone so important to his brother that she gets to call him Eunjae when nobody else does. And the first time they met, he was a complete ass. And she's waiting very patiently for him to get a grip, which reminds him of Ari. And god, he really messed up with Ari. And Jungwoo thinks he might faint. They do it all the time in dramas. Will it cause permanent brain damage? Will he still be able to write songs?

"Jungwoo," says Jiyeon, for maybe the third time. "Are you okay?"

"No," he blurts out. "I'm really not!"

In a rush, Jungwoo gives her the thing he brought all the way from Seoul. He didn't have a lot of time to pack, but deciding which one to take was pretty easy. This is Ari's favorite, the first he ever bought on his own, with the embroidered strap that he found in Barcelona. The lens he uses most is still attached.

"Ari's camera," Jungwoo explains. "The Nikon. I couldn't find the lens cap, I think he lost that when we went to Tokyo Disney last year. But I checked and nothing happened to it on the flight here, see? Just like he left it."

Jiyeon peers into the camera bag, and then she smiles at Jungwoo, so pleased that you might think it was her special treasure he'd carried here in his luggage. "He'll be so excited," she says. "You should give it to him yourself, though. Want me to go get him?"

She has a dimple in her left cheek and a smile that lights up her whole face. Jiyeon wasn't smiling at all, when Jungwoo first met her.

You can keep your money. We'll keep Eunjae. How fiercely she protected his brother. How fiercely Jungwoo did the opposite.

He pushes the camera bag more firmly into her grasp. "No, it's okay. I'll... I'll talk to him some other time. It's a long flight back. I can wait until then." Apollo hasn't set a departure date, but that's not important.

"Hmm."

"And it's been hard to catch him, since I've been so busy. Writing and all that. A lot of writing." That's a lie. He's been stuck ever since Ari disappeared and the block only gets worse by the day. "And he's been with you, which is fair. He should spend as much time with you as he can."

"You can catch Eunjae at breakfast," Jiyeon points out. "Lunch. Dinner. Never misses a meal. None of you do."

"There's too much to talk about. And too many people listening."

"Hmm."

Jungwoo starts inching his way out of the laundry room. "So, um, thanks. For taking that to Ari for me. And I'm... I'm sorry about before. That night, you know. I was upset. It's no excuse, but... Jiyeon, I'm sorry."

Uninvited, Hazel crashes into his head. *You'll apologize to her, but not to me? What the fuck, honestly?*

"It's okay," says Jiyeon, with a sigh. "We can start again, can't we?"

These days, Jungwoo's wanted nothing more than to start again. But even imagining a do-over leaves him paralyzed, sleepless in his bed. What if he got the chance to go back and he just did everything the same way, made the same mistakes, fell victim to the same fears that brought him to where he is right now? And yet, when she bows and introduces herself — *I'm Jiyeon, it's good to meet you* — Jungwoo manages to avoid overthinking it. He performs his part as if their previous meeting never happened, feeling lighter afterward.

"I'll give this to Eunjae, but I hope you'll talk to him soon. When you're ready. He misses you."

Ari misses him? What's there to miss? Jungwoo struggles to believe it. All the cruelties he inflicted, big and small. All the awful words that came not from any muse but from his own terrified heart. How could Ari miss him, after that?"

"Can I ask for your help with something, though?"

He stands up straighter. "You need my help? What can I do?"

Jiyeon's gaze travels beyond him, to the door at the far end of the hall. "You can talk to Max. Just about everyone's had a turn. I told Eunjae I'd try, so that's what I was about to do when you guys called me over, but I think it has to be you."

Jungwoo could cry. Why did she pick an impossible task?

"Look, I know you haven't been around us for very long yet, so I'll go ahead and tell you that I'm Max's least favorite person. That's true most of the time, but especially right now. I don't think I can do you any good, there."

"But I think you can," Jiyeon insists. "He's waiting for you to yell at him, or pick a fight. Maybe both. He might even be thinking that this is something you'll never forgive."

Jungwoo has to scoff at that notion. "I can't say it didn't hurt. It still does. But if he thinks this is the reason it's over between me and Hazel, he's wrong. Max can't take the credit for that one. We've been done for a while," he mumbles, glancing away, "and we just weren't saying it out loud."

"Max could've gone about it differently," says Jiyeon. "I bet he'd want to start again if someone gave him the chance, just like you."

"He did exactly what a stupid kid would do. You can't blame a kid for being a kid."

"A kid." Jiyeon laughs. "By that logic, aren't you also just a kid? Max is only a year younger than you, right?"

"Hey, a year is a lot! I was born in March and Ari's birthday is in July, but even those few months between us make me feel way older most of the time."

"Uh-huh. And I was born in January, which makes me older than both of you. From where I'm standing, you're the kids."

Jungwoo stares at her. "Ari went all in for a noona romance?"

"Noona romance. What do you mean?"

"Nothing! Nothing at all! Forget I said anything!" He needs to talk to Ari! He needs details!

"About Max," Jungwoo says, forcing himself to refocus, "I can't even say I'm really mad at him. Hazel hurt me more than he did. He lied and claimed they were dating, sure, but she's the one who confirmed it. She didn't have to do that. Max expected her to deny it and I guess I did, too." He fidgets with the strap of his watch. "Besides, the fans will punish him enough. It'll get a lot worse before it gets better."

Jiyeon leans against the dryer, holding the camera bag in her arms. The wry humor has evaporated from her expression. "It sounds like you're angrier with Hazel, or putting more blame on her, and I don't think that's fair. Don't go easier on Max just 'cause you think of him as your brother or a kid. He's not a kid, and Hazel never asked to get dragged into this, did she?"

"No," Jungwoo concedes. "She didn't. I think... it's just that no one's ever ended things with me, before. It was always the other way around. I don't know how to deal with it."

"You just deal with it," she replies, not unkindly. "That's never a fun experience, even when it's mutual. It sucks. Try to be fair, anyway." Jiyeon slings the camera bag over her shoulder. A touch of humor returns to her voice. "I have an older sister, Janie, and she likes to say that we can all try to be nice to each other. We used to argue because I've always thought that being fair is better than being nice."

"Being fair is harder than being nice."

"That's true. And sometimes it means you can't be nice." She steps into the hall. "Will you talk to him?"

"I can, but what would I even say?"

"Maybe you can start with everything you just said to me."

Jungwoo decides to try, although there's a high chance that he and Max will end up conducting this conversation (shouting match) through a closed door. But before that, Jungwoo has one more thing to tell her. It's important.

"Don't hurt him," says Jungwoo. "Please." And he knows she understands what — and who — he means. The sudden silence says so much.

"I might, though," Jiyeon replies, quietly. "And he might hurt me. That's how love is. You can't just be there for the good times. You have to stay for everything else, too. And you stay because, no matter what, that person is worth it."

If Jungwoo comes away from this encounter with anything more to ponder, he'll never sleep again. "Is that from your sister, too?"

She smiles, shaking her head. "No. I got that one from my parents."

That's how love is. Jungwoo turns her words over in his head as Ari enters the hallway, looking for Jiyeon. He sees them and lifts a hand in greeting.

"He's gonna try talking to Max," says Jiyeon.

Ari starts walking over right away. "I can go with you, hyung."

"No, it's fine. I've got it." He can handle this. He can stick around for the good things and the bad things. He's late, but he'll start right now.

Jungwoo takes a breath and knocks on Max's door.

The recording is grainy, taken in a room where the only light sources are the TV and a wall sconce shaped like a cactus. Based on the date and time, it was filmed during Apollo's stay at a resort hotel about an hour away from the Los Angeles neighborhood of Lemon Grove.

It's easy to tell that the person filming is Kei. The legs shown in the frame are encased in silk pajama pants and crossed at the ankles. And who else in Apollo would wear suede loafers as house shoes? The others tend to shuffle around in slides and crew socks. Even Kazu has been using some dollar store flip flops, never missing a chance to explain why they were a phenomenal deal. Meanwhile, these pajamas are Dior. And the loafers are also Dior, because Kei never mixes fashion houses. Are you insane?

Jesse twirls into view, also in a matching pajama set. It's safe to assume that this outfit is stolen. Or, if you prefer to use his terminology, borrowed. Not from Kei; these are Vuitton.

"Okay, is it starting? Are we doing it now?" He flops onto the bed, ready with his sheet mask and a pillow, right on top of Kei's legs. "Let's skip the intro, hyung. I can record that some other time."

Kei wriggles away, making an exasperated noise. "Why do you even need me here? You can hold the phone and record it yourself."

"You're better at it though," Jesse whines.

"Better at holding a phone? Pressing a button?"

"Yep! Those things! And Nicky left to go to the gym with Zuzu-hyung, so who else would do it? Gotta be you. Hello?" Jesse doesn't give his brother any time to counter with further argument. He calls out, "Captaaaaaaiiinnnn! Time for another videooooooo!"

"Lower the volume, Ahn. I'm right here."

Jesse shrieks. When did Denny show up? How long has he been sitting in that chair by the window? Even Kei is caught unprepared.

"C-Captain!" he stammers. "Permission to begin, Captain!"

"Granted." Denny folds his arms over his chest. "Reluctantly. What nonsense am I watching this time?"

"Okay, okay. Okay! Here we go. It's the music video for *Trickster*!" Jesse rolls over onto his stomach, skinny legs kicking the air. "Did you know this is like, our most popular video? It has sooooo many views, Boss." He giggles. "Oh my gosh. You'll see why!" More giggling. "Ohhh my gooossshhhh—"

"We worked with a new director," Kei chimes in, because Jesse can't stop giggling long enough to give a proper introduction, "and we've worked with her ever since. She also did *Love Me Leave Me* and *Never Too Late*."

"Oh, and the music video for Keiichi's dark prince agony song!"

This sentence has Denny staring at them in utter bafflement. "Dark prince agony song." He pronounces the words like they're in a foreign language, a string of incomprehensible phonetic sounds.

"Hyung, what anime was that from again? Like, what was the title? It's so long, I can never remember the whole thing. *A Flame of Feathers* and something-something."

Kei uncrosses his ankles. Then he crosses the left over the right, and the right over the left. Opting to ignore Jesse's question, he says, "Let's just start the video."

TRICKSTER (2022)

Clouds brood on a horizon the color of cold iron. Down below, two figures run to meet each other on a vast, windswept moor. Just before they collide, the scene fractures into five-second shots of each Apollo member. Here is Jesse on horseback, galloping to the crest of a hill. A ruffled cravat foams out of the placket of his dress shirt, half untied. Kei contemplates a stained glass window, turning only at the final second. His coat is McQueen and the brooch is a vintage piece on loan from Cartier. Meanwhile, Max hesitates in front of a fortune teller's wagon, his top half draped in voluminous white linen. As for the bottom half, those leather pants had to have been painted on.

[PAUSE]

Denny lifts an eyebrow. "And he needs two belts...why?"

"For the vibes, Captain. Remember? We talked about this?"

"Those pants don't need any help staying on. The belts are extraneous. They have zero utility."

"The belts," Jesse says, "are an *aesthetic*." He explains this slowly, as though teaching the alphabet to a toddler. "And aren't you going to say anything about me? Look at how I came in on a horse. Did you know everybody else fell off theirs? Not me, though. I did it perfectly."

A snort from Denny. "So you can't handle your own two legs, but you show improvement if we add four more. Understood."

The middle brothers are next. Ari stands framed in the shadow of a stone arch, his attention drawn to something off-screen. He's grown out his hair just a bit. That's a tartan trench from Burberry, Black Watch, with a thistle threaded through the second button. We switch to Jungwoo in an oxblood blazer, lying on the floor as tarot cards rain down in drifts. The one that lands on his chest is the Tower, reversed. And when we leave him there in the candlelight, we find Namgyu slumped on a bench at a train station. He holds a bouquet of red roses and one suspender strap has slipped free. His face is wet with tears.

[PAUSE]

"What's with Hong being the saddest one in every video?" Denny demands to know. Jesse's response is to roll onto his back, giggling some more.

Kei says, "I think it's because the fans get so emotional over him."

"So they like seeing him cry...?"

For some deep and portentous reason, Apollo's oldest members are all on the move. Nicky leaps over a weathered fence, plunging into a meadow where the grass sways waist high. He's in a muslin shirt with a high, banded collar. Why is the sleeve torn from elbow to wrist? Why does he have an artfully placed wound on his cheek? And then there's Kazu, who might not be wearing a shirt at all. We catch flashes of his sculpted chest as he races down a row of theater seats, displacing women in evening gowns and men in suits. His black wool coat hangs open, some of the buttons dangling by a thread.

Last, of course, is Jaehwan. He's out on the moors, no coat, in a silk shirt that billows in the wind. This bleak backdrop only serves to make his beauty seem all the more luminous. The music swells, a torrent of violins, the crash of thunder. He falls to his knees. We hear these lines narrated in English: You changed your heart. I'll change my fate. *The first is read by Max. The second is read by Ari.*

The screen goes dark. Text materializes in a seductive, curling script: TRICKSTER: APOLLO.

[PAUSE]

"Alright, what historical period is this supposed to be?" Denny gestures at the screen. "We've got t-shirts, trench coats, and basically everything someone might wear if they were dying of consumption in the 1800s. There's a wagon. This lady's in a cape and Lee looks like an extra on that one ride at Disney, with the boat and the sea shanties." He snaps his fingers. "*Pirates of the Caribbean.*"

"Oh my gosh!!! Oh myyyy gggooossshhh Max really dooeeessss!!!" Jesse, who was already giggling, is now laughing so hard he can barely breathe. Somewhere in there, he might have said, 'Captain Max Sparrow' while snorting into his pillow.

"And the one from the Tokyo crime syndicate, what's his deal? Why isn't he ever wearing a complete set of clothing?"

Kei throws the remote onto the bed. "That's what I've been saying!"

Between dance cuts in a rose garden, Ari skids down a steep riverbank. He's lost the beautiful trench coat and is down to a white tee tucked into black trousers. The hems are bedraggled, the shirt shredded as though he came charging through a wall of thorns to reach this place. The camera swings behind him to show that he's trying to catch up to a woman in a red dress. Played by actress Hazel Lim, the song's titular trickster goes crashing right into the water. Ari dives in after her. Although she turns around to shout at him, he snatches her up in his arms and holds her tight, both of them waist-deep in the river—

[PAUSE]

Gawking at the screen, Jesse exclaims, "Wait! Hyung, did you skip that far ahead? This part doesn't even happen until close to the end."

"I didn't do anything," Kei replies, equally flabbergasted. He picks up the remote and rewinds to the part where Jaehwan is on his knees. Then he nudges the video forward again. But no matter what he does, it jumps straight from the opening to this scene between Ari and Hazel, like the video has been rearranged. Because, of course, it has.

Kei points at Jesse. "You got this from Nicky, didn't you?"

"Got what from Nicky? The video? I mean, he sent me that link this morning and said, 'Listen, Jess. Just hear me out. Wouldn't it be so funny if you had the Captain watch *Trickster* today? You know, for the reaction videos you've been making? Think about it. Good idea, right?' And I said I would, because it *is* funny—"

There's a sound like a dozen boulders rolling down a hillside, or perhaps a glacier calving into the Arctic Sea. Denny is on his feet and the chair has tumbled sideways onto the floor. Is he laughing? Roaring? Jesse's instinct is to seek shelter. He burrows under the covers with a squeal of terror. Kei loses his grip on the phone, probably because

Jesse kicked him in the ribs by accident. With the camera knocked face down onto the bed, all we get is the audio.

"What is Ryan doing?"

"N-nothing! It was just pretend!"

"That was in the script," Kei hurries to tell him, although later he'll wonder why he worked so hard to prevent Ari from getting crushed to a pulp in Denny's enormous fists. Maybe that idiot kind of deserves it, after everything he put them through. Nevertheless, he dives for the remote and tries to skip to a part of the video that is safer, less incendiary.

The current is strong and Ari's white shirt is plastered to his skin, clinging in all the right places—

Jesse goes back to screeching. Kei keeps skipping forward, and now Denny has his own phone out, he's punching a number on speed dial—

— clinging in all the right places. Hazel has one hand curved around the back of his neck, face turned up as if waiting for a kiss.

"Waaaahhhh, Nicky sabotaged the whole thing, the rest of it is just Ari's scene over and over again!"

Jesse explodes out of the tangle of sheets and blankets, grabs the remote, and turns the TV off. He manages to do this just before the music video gives way to a series of quotes pulled from YouTube comments, social media posts, Sunshine reaction videos, and Wattpad serials with very mature ratings. The quotes could best be described in modern language as 'thirsty.' It's hard to tell if Denny is more offended by the words or by Nicky's choice to type everything out in Comic Sans.

Jesse commences pleading with the Captain for Ari-hyung's life. Swearing a litany of oaths in Japanese, Kei remembers the phone and stops the recording.

[PAUSE]

"Okay, okay, okay. Okay. This is the right video, now. The *real* video."

The room has been restored to order. We might never know the fate of Jesse's sheet mask, but every piece of furniture is upright again, and Denny is back in his chair. He eyes the screen with overt suspicion.

Kei sighs. "Let's try again."

We follow Hazel into a ballroom crowded with dancers in gilded masks. She flies from one Apollo member to the next in a whirl of dark curls and blood-red chiffon. Only Namgyu manages to keep her for long; he sweeps Hazel into a dizzying foxtrot as the song builds up to its chorus. They make it look like it's the easiest thing in the world. She doesn't stay with Namgyu, though. Eventually, she plants a kiss on his cheek and leaves him bereft.

[PAUSE]

"Hazel asked the director if she could do this ballroom part with Gyu," says Jesse, "but none of us had taken any classes yet, like not until we were getting ready for *Love Me Leave Me*. So Jaehwan told Namgyu-hyung that the ballroom dancing was a game."

Kei nods. "You can get him to master just about anything if you say it's a game. He loves games."

"Hyung's weirdly good at them. It's just so crazy. Like, did you know he speaks Japanese almost as well as Zu and Keiichi? And he wasn't even born there. Oh! And Spanish, too. Fluent. We put him on that one app with the owl that stalks you if you don't do the lessons."

"Interesting," says Denny. "And this works for any skill?"

"Yeah. We really need to do that again, but with English this time."

"A game..." If you're very, very quiet, you can hear the cogs turning in Denny's head. "Hang on, let me make some notes..."

As Hazel slips through Jungwoo's fingers next, laughing, we can't help comparing this character with the one she plays on the silver screen. Hazel filmed for Trickster *only two short months before production began on the movie that would change the trajectory of her career. Now, most of the world knows her as ruthless assassin Gretchen Young. Before that, though, Sunshines knew her as the woman who delivered a roundhouse kick directly to Kazu's chest, nearly toppling him from his private box and into the orchestra—*

[PAUSE]

"Play that part again."

Kei complies with the Captain's order. Hazel's action sequence unfolds two more times.

"Huh," says Denny. "Nice form. Lee should ask her for lessons."

"Oh my gosh," Jesse wheezes. "Ohhhh my gooossshhh."

Max stares at the fortune teller's wagon. The loose linen shirt slips down one shoulder and a lock of hair tumbles into his eyes. His cheeks are flushed with cold. Then he disappears into the wagon's interior, a narrow space illuminated by the glow of a crystal ball. Bundles of herbs and dried flowers hang from hooks in the sloped ceiling.

Max takes a seat in front of Hazel, still looking like he might bolt at any second. She reaches out to read his palm, but he ends up taking both of her hands in his. If Hazel is startled by this, it doesn't show. She only smiles. Light swells from the crystal ball... and then, it shatters.

[PAUSE]

"Ohhh myyy gooosssshhhhhh." Jesse starts rolling around on the bed, giggling like he'll never stop. "Can you believe him? Can you really believe he's dating her? What was he thinking, why did he do that?"

"There wasn't any thinking involved," Kei replies.

"But I just... I just realized..." The rolling turns into a fit of laughter so severe that Denny opens his mouth, about to remind Jesse that breathing is mandatory for survival. "I just... hyung, don't you see... that it was Jungwoo stealing Jaehwan's girl all along... because he keeps dating the ones in the music videos... like, it was Ruby and then Hazel... so what Max did, was it actually..." More laughing. "Was it actually," Jesse croaks, "just karma???"

"Idiot," whispers Kei, but who's to say which brother he's referring to?

In pursuit of Hazel, Ari tears through the fog and into a freezing river. Although she turns around to shout at him, he snatches her up in his arms and holds her tight. The current is strong, threatening to drag them both under, and Ari's white shirt is soaked through. He won't let go no matter how ferociously she fights, and eventually she sags against him with a sob. When she lifts her head, it's to whisper something in Ari's ear. It seems like a kiss is inevitable. But then Hazel presses the cold blade of a knife to the hollow of his throat...

[PAUSE]

Jesse and Kei are powerless to stop Denny from calling their brother on the phone. Ari isn't asleep yet, or else it would just go to voicemail; no one can wake him once he's out. The younger brothers scurry over to eavesdrop. Yes, even Kei. If Apollo's about to lose a member permanently, doesn't he have a right to know?

"RYAN," Denny thunders into the receiver.

"Boss," says Ari. According to the captions, it sounds like he's outdoors, with a particularly loud cricket nearby. "Ah, what's wrong? Everything okay?"

"How could you do this?"

"How could I do what...? What happened...?"

Denny's nostrils flare. "This!" he shouts back, motioning at the image frozen on the TV screen: Ari and Hazel in the river, entwined in a deadly embrace. "You've gotta be kidding me. How can your eyes be this empty?"

"I don't...? Woosung-ah, I'm not sure what I did, but I'm really sorry—"

"Every time I think you've made progress—"

"Um, and you know I can't see what you're pointing at, if you're pointing at something. I think that you are...?"

But now someone else has taken over the call. "Why are you yelling at him?" Jiyeon demands. "Yell at me instead."

"Give the phone back to Ryan," says Denny, fuming. "Ryan! I know you can hear me! The signs were all there! It's like I've taught you nothing. HOW DID YOU FAIL TO NOTICE THAT THIS WOMAN WAS ARMED—"

And this, dear Sunshines, is where the video ends.

Rules

Kei

K EI WAS A PRINCE once. The others have never allowed him to forget it.

To be clear, he provided the voice acting — speaking and singing — for the prince in an anime. It was about war-torn lands and star-crossed love. He performed the role just one time, but his brothers resurrect the joke whenever he seems to be making a princely request: that specific orange juice brand from the supermarket, or the sequined pants hemmed to this exact length before he has to wear them on stage. And Kei knows, as the clock rolls over from 12:01 to 12:02, that he'll be accused of issuing royal commands the instant he complains about Max and Jungwoo waking him up.

He does it anyway. Idiots!

"Can you guys please shut the hell up?"

His brothers continue staring each other down. The door to the bungalow is already partway open, a bar of moonlight bisecting the room, and Jungwoo has one foot over the threshold. He seems prepared to make a stormy exit. Max is gearing up to prevent this from happening. Kei throws a pillow at him, intercepting the flying tackle before it can happen.

"Ya! Go to bed! Why are you so obsessed with each other?"

"Calm down, Keiichi," Jungwoo replies. "It's fine. We're done here."

They don't look like they're done. Max confirms as much, in language as colorful and offensive as the hoodie-and-pajamas ensemble he's wearing. He stops even trying to keep his voice down, not that the furious whispering was really very quiet to begin with. Kei can only be grateful that Jungwoo chooses not to engage. He just blows out of the room, letting the screen door bang shut behind him. Kei kicks the sheets aside and latches onto Max.

Some people start fights and don't finish them. Max can start a fight and never let it end. In fact, he can start multiple fights in tandem and then juggle all of these with the panache of a circus performer on stilts.

Kei drags him away from the door. It blows his mind that Max and Jungwoo might end up locked in eternal conflict over a girl. It might be different if one or the other was actually in love with Hazel, but it seems to Kei that she's just caught in the crossfire with the rest of them.

"Drop it," he hisses. "I'm serious. Why are you even fighting again? What the hell is left to fight about at this point?"

Max wrenches his arm free. "You know fuck-all about this mess," he says, hoarse from too much arguing, "so just stay out of it. Go back to bed."

"It's hard to stay out of it when you guys decide to bring your melodramatic bullshit into the room where I'm trying to sleep." And he has more to say, ever so much more, but now Max is collecting his stuff like he's going somewhere, picking out what he needs by the weak light of his phone screen. It's as if he has no notion of how late it is. The hills surrounding the resort are dark, jagged shapes set against an even darker sky. There's nothing open right now; Kei would wager that the lodge at the center of the property is the only place Max could go.

Or so he thinks, until he realizes that his brother has claimed an extra pair of keys. They jingle softly on a keychain shaped like a lemon. Kei has seen Denny toting these around often enough to know that the yellow enamel is scratched, and the rental company's phone number is on the reverse, printed on a peeling label.

"Where are you going?" he demands, trailing Max outdoors in a fugue of disbelief. The guy's lost his mind. No, scratch that. Everyone's lost their minds, this summer.

Kei wants to scream but is too refined to give in to that compulsion. He watches his brother stomp away, crushing a froth of pink blossoms underfoot, a hoodlum in hideous polyester pajamas. Left behind, Kei bristles at the familiar humming and whirring of his conscience going into overdrive. This isn't allowed, it reminds him. He's breaking the rules.

Kei is not a rule breaker. No wonder Max left without a backward glance. The last thing he expects is for Kei to chase him down. And yet, what if something bad happens?

Safety beckons. Compliance is a siren song. And Kei does retreat, heading back inside to the tune of a midnight chorus: the tremulous melody of a cricket, and wind chimes ringing from the porch next door. He resists the urge to change into more appropriate attire, since he doesn't have time. Kei's sole concession to decorum is a sweater that he throws on in a hurry. Then he steps out again, feeling like the worst felon on earth. Underdressed: check. Out after mandated curfew: check.

He breaks into a jog, wishing he knew of a shortcut. Kei hasn't gone anywhere except the main lodge and his own bunk. They've only been here since mid-morning, moved to this resort after a perimeter breach at the last safehouse. How those Sunshines contrived to find them is still a mystery.

Although he wants to call out to Max, Kei just pelts after him instead. He rushes past the other bungalows, identical and linked to theirs by gravel pathways that snake across the property, silver ribbons under a full, round moon. The air is clear, even a little brisk at this slightly higher altitude, and every sound carries. He doesn't want to be the reason anybody else wakes up, especially Denny. At least one member of this group should make an effort. Eight guys who need to be fed, housed, and hidden from view — they're such an inconvenience.

At this rate, the Captain will leave them. And they need

Denny because the alternative is living in a vortex of chaos, liberated from even the semblance of structure. He already refers to them as a clown brigade, a nonsense marathon, a disaster-hydra with eight heads that just keep growing back. Kei can barely live that down as it is. What an embarrassment. Perhaps the only source of greater mortification is his memory of confessing — as the anime prince — that the enemy had become his lover.

He doesn't catch up to Max and his loping stride until the parking area is in sight. It's just about empty, as mundane as mundane can be, and yet it bothers him to look at it. There are no lines striping the asphalt, no neat boxes marking where you should park. Kei's brain takes it as another reminder that this is what they've chosen for themselves: anarchy. A rudderless jaunt into the unknown.

Kei sprints over to the van just as Max is climbing in. He seizes the door handle, resulting in a tug-of-war, but they're evenly matched in strength. Max keeps it from ending in a draw by extending one long leg and threatening to stamp a shoe print into Kei's chest. A shoe print! On this sweater!

He shoves Max's foot away. "This is Dior," he seethes. "Don't you dare."

"Sorry, Your Highness," Max seethes back at him. "Should've aimed for your face instead."

Kei spots the keys in his brother's free hand. He darts forward and swipes them. Victorious, he motions for Max to get out. "Game over. Let's go."

"Fuck right off, Keiichi."

"Same to you. Get out."

"Or what? You'll go fully *Grand Theft Auto* on my ass? Please do, it'd be the funniest thing you've ever done in your whole life—" Max snaps his mouth shut. Voices drift past, carried on a gust of wind. Beyond the parking lot's bounds, two people wend their way toward the bungalows at a leisurely pace, bearing a laundry basket between them.

Kei swears under his breath. "That's Ari-hyung," he mutters. Doing laundry in the dead of night. Laughing with his secret girlfriend under the stars. Insane! Everyone and everything has gone completely insane!

"Don't," says Max.

"Don't what?"

"Don't go over there!"

"I wasn't planning on going over there!"

"Yeah, right. You were thinking about it. And you would've, if I hadn't said anything. You can never just leave it the fuck alone. You can never just let it be."

Kei knows this is true. It stings anyway, to hear it spoken.

This latest bout of arguing reaches a volume high enough to rouse suspicion. Ari hangs back, pausing to look around. Of course he'd be mindful of his surroundings now, when it's too late. This is why the Captain scolds him for his lack of peripheral awareness. Kei almost remarks on it, but the sentence is knocked right out of his brain when Max starts hauling him into the van. All he manages to verbalize is a muffled, "What the hell!"

"Shut up," Max whispers harshly. "They'll see us, moron."

He snatches someone's discarded jacket from the floorboard and uses it to smother the sound of Kei's complaining. They remain this way for an entire minute, jammed in an awkward tangle on the driver's side, a knot of mutual hatred. Kei can't decide which is more insulting: having this thing wrapped around his head or the fact that it's been on the floor for days, trampled and covered in beach sand. The pattern stitched along the cuffs suggests a fashion house that just announced Kazu as an ambassador two months ago, so it probably belongs to him. To be even more specific, it's an expensive garment left to molder in a van, so it probably belonged to Kazu until Jesse stole it.

It occurs to him, sprawled across Max's lap in the front seat, that every Apollo fanfic writer on the Internet would go wild for this scene. Dear god, Kei hates it here.

The threat passes. They lapse into a brief, poisonous silence. Max finds no resistance when he attempts to reclaim the keys; Kei is too preoccupied with collecting the tattered remnants of his dignity. That, and shaking sand out of Kazu's poor, ill-treated bomber jacket. *I don't care anymore*, he tries to tell himself. *He wants me to let it be? Fine. I'll fucking let it be.* And when his brother starts the engine, Kei is still committed to ignoring him. Never mind that Max's dumb choices have the potential to reverberate throughout multiple lives, including Kei's; he's not about to waste any more of his time, tonight.

Headlights flare. Wheels crunch on the pavement. Kei bundles the jacket into his arms, wondering if there's any chance he can have it dry-cleaned in the morning. Then, he hears a tortured sigh. Max has rolled the window down. "Come on," he calls out to Kei. "Get in the stupid car."

Kei whips around. "What? No."

"Get in or I'll honk the horn until Denny comes out here."

"Why should I have to die when you do?" Kei exclaims, aghast. Max responds by raising his hand over the steering wheel in a wordless threat. Since the horn would undoubtedly be the last sound either of them ever heard, once Denny was through with them, Kei finds himself outmatched yet again. He climbs into the van feeling as rumpled and abused as Kazu's jacket.

A meandering drive connects the resort to the highway. The approach was so long, coming in from the city, that Kei began to wonder if they'd ever arrive. The road seems even longer now. It winds away from the lodge and its cluster of bungalows, past outbuildings and slumbering machinery. Max hangs left at the first intersection instead of steering down the route that Kei remembers. Overhanging boughs dip down to rasp against the roof. It's too dark to read the sign mounted on a post, but it turns out there's no need for it. Soon enough, the landscape fills with citrus groves laid out in tidy rows.

When Max pulls into a small picnic area, Kei is quick to jump out. He goes straight to the fence, curling his fingers over the worn wood, trying to take everything in at once. Lemon trees march along both sides of the road. Moonlight drips from every leaf. Blossoms still linger here and there, although spring is long gone and summer is more than halfway over. The scent of them sweetens the air.

Kei did notice brochures on display at the lodge, glossy pamphlets inviting guests on Instagram-worthy excursions: touring fields of wildflowers, picking their own fruit. He recalls the Captain mentioning that this place doubles as a working farm, though he didn't think much more about it afterward, and he never guessed that the groves were so close by.

Kei leans against the fence, saying nothing when Max joins him a moment later. So peaceful is the view that a measure of his earlier fury just melts away. Everything is in order, here. The lanes between rows are evenly spaced, so satisfying to look at. Tools are ready and waiting to be used again tomorrow. Crates have been stacked, ladders propped against trunks. Kei didn't expect to find comfort, roped into delinquency with Max, but he can't deny that being here is soothing.

"It's nice," he murmurs. An understatement, but he feels inadequate to the task of describing how he really feels about it.

Max nods, resting his forearms on the top rail. "Saw the sign on my way back, earlier. I wanted to come see. Wasn't planning on it being the middle of the night, but it is what it is."

"On your way back from where?" He didn't even know that Max left.

"My sister's in town. Denny let me take the van so I could go see her, since she flies out again tomorrow." Max fidgets with the lemon keychain. "Well, it's today, I guess. Since it's so late now."

"You should've given the keys back when you were done," Kei admonishes him, the words coming out automatically. Then he recognizes that he's defaulted to nagging. To make up for this, he mumbles, "Which sister?"

Holding up two fingers, Max replies, "The second. Mikaela."

Kei angles his face away so that he can't be caught frowning. Max is the youngest of four, with three older sisters. The first two are in love with Kazu, of all people. The third prefers Ari. They've been nothing but kind during the few occasions he's met them in person, but if these ladies had any sense, they'd pick Jaehwan.

"Shit, I said I'd get some pictures. Kaela used to work at a place like this when she was in high school. Grapefruit, not lemons. She'd answer the phones and send out invoices." Max drops the car keys into the pocket of his hoodie, swapping them for his phone. He aims the camera at the trees, angling up to include a slice of star-strewn sky. Shaking his head, he adds, "I used to get so fucking tired of grapefruit."

"Is this the sister who teaches yoga?"

"Pilates. And no, that's Mackenzie. Mikaela's an accountant." Max swipes through the photos he's taken, then chooses one to send. "She was in LA for work again. I missed her last time she was here, in June, but it's not like I could just go out for lunch in the middle of... you know."

"In the middle of hyung running away to become a waffle seller."

"Don't be shitty about it, Keiichi."

"I'm not! The Captain is a waffle seller, isn't he? I'm just pointing out that none of us could do anything or go anywhere, and it was because of Ari."

"We can go anywhere now. That's because of Ari, too."

Kei's not about to dispute this. He understands that things couldn't be left the way they were. When it comes to the contract, he's grateful for what Ari did. And he's been trying so hard to bury his anxiety, to pretend that he's as hopeful about the future as his brothers seem to be. But here is the situation: they have no agency. Nor can they agree on an offer to accept, from the ones they've received thus far. Things are further complicated by Sunshines demanding Max's head on a silver platter for dating Hazel Lim. The entire industry is watching as Emerald's stocks keep plummeting in the aftermath of Apollo's departure, and now everyone on earth seems to know the humiliating truth: all nine of them were too stupid for words. All nine of them signed those contracts without asking enough questions.

They were duped. Swindled. Kei has no clue how to even begin preparing for what might be the end of their collective careers. He made the choice to give everything to this dream when he was scarcely fourteen years old. No part of that investment is refundable, no part of their future is certain, so why is he the only one worried about what's next? Shouldn't they all be panicking?

"I think we were right to leave Emerald," he tells Max, "but we should've stopped there. Everyone should've stopped there. We don't even know if we can recover from this." His anger starts to surge again. The peace he found in this place is rapidly disintegrating. "Why did you do it? There was no call for you to fuck with Jungwoo on that level. We didn't need to be in the news for one more damn thing. Now we've got fans who want you out of the group."

"It won't come to that."

"You seem so fucking sure."

"Because I am. This is temporary. And why do *you* seem so fucking sure that this is my fault and nobody else's?"

Temporary? In what way? Kei can only bark out a laugh. "Who came up with that half-assed revenge plan? Wasn't it you, idiot?"

"She was supposed to deny it," Max all but shouts at him. "That was the plan, not this!"

"Half-assed!" Kei maintains, unmoved. "You didn't even go into it with your whole ass! How the hell did you think that would turn out? But you never think, that's the fucking problem."

"Yeah, I could've thought about it harder. I won't argue with that. You know what else, though? It was a chance for Jungwoo to step up, and he refused. He couldn't even own the fact that Hazel was his girlfriend and not mine." Max turns his head to glare at Kei. "What I did was wrong. But don't forget that Jungwoo had no plans to ever make it right."

"How was he supposed to make it right? By admitting that he'd been seeing her for months? There couldn't be a worse time to do that. I get what you're saying, but I understand him, too. Jungwoo knows the rules. Even Ari knows the rules. That's why he's decided to keep it quiet." He sees no reason to expound further because they both know what those rules are, and foremost among them is this: no dating. They belong to their fans.

"And what if breaking the rules helps someone else? Should we still follow them anyway?"

Kei doesn't have a simple answer, no matter how simple it seems to Max. Rules exist for a reason, right? A lot of them appear pointless or incomprehensible on the surface, but most are there to ensure that people don't get hurt. The same can't really be said for breaking them. Kei won't go so far as to say that there are never exceptions, but he isn't like Max. He can only be himself: questioning his brothers' choices, terrified of the direction he might be forced to go just because nine years ago, they all agreed to walk together.

They're quiet again on the drive back, both mired in their own thoughts. Max punches the brake a bit too hard when they pull into their space in the parking lot, and Kei glances up to see Ari waiting there, sitting on the sidewalk next to Jiyeon. They come over to the van as Max cuts the engine.

"Hyung," he says, abashed. "Emma-noona."

Ari looks from Max to Kei, then back to Max again. "Please tell me Denny knows you borrowed the car."

"Why does everyone think I'd be stupid enough to cross Denny?"

Kei gawks at him. "Because you're stupid enough to go public with an actress you've met three times! We're just being logical!"

"He said I could have the keys," Max explains to their brother, ignoring everything Kei just said. "I hadn't given them back yet, and Jungwoo-hyung pissed me off, so I left. I needed..." The words taper off. "I needed to think. That's all."

"He shouldn't have been driving when he was upset." Kei

thinks that Ari needs to hear the whole story. He's still the oldest brother present, which gives him authority even though he's devolved into a lovelorn idiot.

"I would've been fine," Max insists. "I have a license. I know how to drive. This jackass didn't need to come after me like I'd end up in a ditch as soon as I hit the gas pedal."

Ari considers this. Then he says, "Kei went with you because he was worried. He didn't want you to get hurt." Gently, he takes the keys from Max. "You both got back okay, so let's just leave it at that."

"Hmm, I thought the story would be more exciting," muses Jiyeon. "*Florida man steals vehicle loaded with ten cases of plastic boba straws. Still at large.*"

Even though Kei doesn't quite get the joke — must be some weird American thing — the meaning is certainly not lost on Max. He turns to Jiyeon, eyes wide, like she just dumped a gallon of ice water on his head and ran away snickering. "Noona, goddamn!"

"Sorry. I had to do it." Laughing now, she adds, "No more Florida man jokes until next week, I promise."

Max goes back to Ari, at a loss. "I thought she liked me!"

"She does," their brother replies, but he can't keep a straight face, and even Kei starts to lose it along with him. It's just so fulfilling to watch Max Lee scrape his jaw off the asphalt. The last time he displayed this level of indignation was when a Malaysian magazine managed to acquire some baby photos, voluntarily and lovingly curated by his eldest sister, Madison.

Maybe this is what it's like to have sisters. A pale imitation, no doubt, but also an interesting change of pace. Maybe sisters just tease you about being from Florida instead of hiding your left shoe every morning for six days straight, or re-enacting only the sappiest scenes from your stint as Adrianos, dark mage-prince of the Lunar Fells.

Kei only knows about having too many brothers. They roll into your room without knocking, borrow your expensive moisturizer without asking. They memorize the lyrics of an award-winning ballad that you sang, as Prince Adrianos, to a beautiful griffin-shifter queen named Lyranel the Ever-Golden. Then they sing that ballad to everyone in the Emerald Entertainment cafeteria, wearing wigs and cheap capes they ordered online. Jesse always wants to play Lyranel, who brandishes a knife at Adrianos right before fainting in a graceful heap at his feet. And Kei is so damn sick of his brothers right now, but as he draws on the peaceful memory of those citrus groves in the moonlight, he finds that Apollo comes to mind as well.

Maybe the groves have shown him why the others can face the future so bravely. Even in the deepest chaos, there are things about Apollo that never change. They're like trees standing side by side in the same row, enduring the same storms. Roots have laced into a tangle underground after so many years growing together.

They aren't growing in the same ways. And yet, despite the perils of uncooperative weather, of pestilence and fire and human error, those trees are still growing. They endure, following a pattern that waxes and wanes. Come what may, the cycle goes on.

Come what may, they just keep reaching for the sun.

The video begins with a view of the ceiling. We can hear Namgyu chattering away at someone, chipper as usual, but he's wandered away from his phone. Indeed, he may have forgotten where he left it.

In the chat, some Sunshines voice confusion. The majority, however, are unsurprised. Regular viewers of his livestreams would be more alarmed if the man actually showed up on time for his own broadcast. It's a few more minutes before we hear Namgyu cry out, "Oh! I was supposed to talk to Sunshines! Where did I put my phone..."

Someone replies, "On the coffee table, hyung."

"Aww! Ari, you're the best, it *is* on the coffee table!" A moment later, Namgyu is waving wildly at the thousands of fans watching through the Star-Connect app. He beams at the camera, effervescent with joy. The sweater is Gucci and the baseball cap, worn backwards, has the word ELEVATOR embroidered on it. We will never know why. Is this the brand? Is it a cryptic message? Does it perhaps make no sense at all and is meant to teach us about the unfathomable mysteries of life?

Regardless, Namgyu is delighted to be here. He can't see his audience, only himself and a chat log with new lines appearing by the second. Even so, he demands to know how everybody got so much prettier. The fans throw this question right back at him.

"Oh, you think I got prettier? Me? Awwwww! You guys, that's so nice!" He pauses to read some more. "I did change my hair," he replies, removing the hat so viewers can see the color more closely. It's gone from strawberry blond to a warm, peachy pink. The chat fills with shrieks of admiration and dozens of emoji: hearts, baby chicks, sparkles, more hearts, crying faces.

"I like it a lot, and the members told me they like it too. Aren't they so nice? The best brothers. I'm so happy!"

>> EEEEEEEEEEEEEEEEE

> > but oppa where are u right now
> > Oppa don't go bald tho :(:(:(
> > omg he just changed his hair for Never
>   Too Late promo and now it's different
>   again!!!!
> > I WANT TO SQUISH HIMMMMMMMMMM
> > hong namgyu just give me 1 chance
> > Where is he?? That's not the dorms

"Where am I? Hey, that's a really great question! Can you guess? Haha!"

Namgyu holds the camera at arm's length, slowly turning so that Sunshines can snoop all they want over his shoulder. We see a living room done up in stylish monochrome, and although the furniture is a bit sparse, every piece radiates comfort: plush rugs, piles of toss pillows, a couch with cushions like fluffy marshmallows. Sliding glass doors open onto a balcony overlooking the city. The hour is late; lights twinkle down below.

In the chat, Sunshines are quick to point out that there are other members of Apollo in the room with Namgyu. Ari and Jungwoo are both here, the latter with his guitar and omnipresent notebook. They wave and say hello. Neither can sit on the couch because it's been claimed by Max; part of his face is covered with a folded washcloth and the rest is covered by a mask, but Sunshines know it's him anyway. That's his favorite hoodie, printed with the name of an American university where his dad attended on a basketball scholarship long ago. He's sprawled across the cushions like a murder victim, long limbs splayed out, occupying every inch of space.

"Aww, you want to know if Max is okay?" Namgyu walks over to the couch and sits beside him. Lowering his voice, he explains, "Our poor Lee Seojin, he's allergic to cats. Isn't that sad? But we gave him medicine! And this is a little towel that we soaked in cold water. He puts it on his eyes to help with the itching. Don't worry about him, Sunshines! Doctor Hong is here!"

We hear muffled noises from underneath the pillow. Ari leans sideways, listening. "Ah, Max says just leave him here to die." He rests a sympathetic hand on Max's shoulder. "Maybe we should head out. You'll feel better."

More muffled noises, most of which are probably expletives. Jungwoo laughs, looking up from his notebook to say, "Sunshines, you know where we are by now, right? The cat should be a big clue."

```
>> JAEHWAN'S APARTMENT
>> goodbye party… omg im so sad!!!! why
   does he have to enlist
>> They're at leader's house!!!
>> omg omg omg omg omg where is he where
```

```
   is kei's cat!!!!!!!!!
>> Masamune MY KING where is he
>> can we please see jaehwan oppa!!!!!
>> Can    we    see    the    cat??????
   Nyansamuneeeeeee
>> Keiichi got a cat and then made his
   mom take care of it lolololol
>> Classic
>> where is keiichi-oppa? is everyone
   there?
```

"Sunshines, you're so smart! You're like detectives!" Namgyu gives Max a pat on the knee. "Feel better, okay? Sunshines wanna see Keiichi-kun so I'll take them there right now! But I'll come back and sit with you some more when I'm done." To the camera, he whispers, "His eyes are all puffed up. Like a goldfish! So cute! So sad!"

Meanwhile, Ari's expression has grown fretful. "Hyung, maybe it's not a good idea to go find Kei right now…"

"Good point," Jungwoo replies. "I mean, listen to them."

"They're only getting louder." Ari brushes at overgrown bangs that keep falling into his eyes. "You know, maybe it's time for all of us to leave. Jaehwan-hyung should get some rest before tomorrow."

Namgyu only laughs. "We can't leave yet! That's so silly! We won't get to see leader-hyung very much anymore, so we can't go until he kicks us out. It's our last chance to be with him for a while!"

"But they're so noisy, hyung. What about the neighbors?"

"Don't you worry about it, Ari. Gosh, you're so sweet, you're always so worried! It'll all be okay. Nobody's calling the cops about Zuzu and Keiichi. Why would you complain about them singing? It sounds amazing!"

With that, Namgyu turns on his heel and exits the living room. Right away, we hear tinny music, the bass a little too pronounced. Two people are singing along to an iconic Japanese pop song about first love. Joining in for the remaining verses, our host progresses down a hallway lined with... trophies? At least a dozen, in different shapes and sizes. Through commentary from Sunshines, we learn that these are Apollo's trophies from various industry award shows and music programs. The group voted to have all of them transferred to Jaehwan's apartment when he moved out of the dorms a few months ago.

"He wants custom shelving for them," Namgyu replies, when fans observe that the trophies are still waiting to be properly displayed. He speaks at a higher volume to be heard above the balladeers in the room ahead. "And he says he wants cabinet doors that close with a remote control so he can hide the trophies and forget that we exist. Isn't that hilarious? Leader-nim is just the funniest, right?"

Near the end of the hall, Namgyu lets out a yelp and

fumbles the phone, catching it just seconds before it hits the ground. We see bare feet and the cuffs of someone's distressed jeans. "Hyung! Didn't see you there! Sorry, sorry! Gottagothoughbyeeeeeee!" And then the feet are gone, sprinting in the opposite direction. Namgyu swings the camera to reveal that this miscreant is Jesse.

"Be careful, you'll fall down!" he calls to him, and Jesse gives a backward wave, striped sweater sleeve flapping in the air.

```
>> LOOOOLLL jesse never out of jail
   stripes
>> he's been in jail stripes for at least
   2 weeks now
>> Nicky too though and tbh FREE MY MAN
>> Omg what did he do
>> JESSE MARRY ME I'M BEGGING
>> The fact that Jaehwan still makes them
   wear stripes when they're busted
>> Those are his prisoners!!
>> lmao been doing that since pre-debut
>> JUST APOLLO THINGS
>> it was smth jess did w nicky right??
>> hwannie let me be ur prisoner :( :(
>> Can't believe bro's grounded again
   like how does he even do this
```

Namgyu says, "Aww you guys, it was so bad. He shouldn't hang out with Nicky so much. They get into all kinds of trouble! But not me. Leader-hyung only put me in stripes one time, after I got lost in Las Vegas. Haha!"

The aforementioned noise is now impossible to ignore. It's coming from the kitchen. But rather than charging straight to its source, Namgyu lingers in the hall. He rotates the phone camera and lowers his voice. "We won't bother them," he tells Sunshines. "They're feeling super sad right now since leader-hyung goes to the army tomorrow. You can say hi another time, okay? Awww."

Jaehwan's kitchen, like his living room, adheres to a minimalist aesthetic. We get the sense that it's normally cleaner than this, though. Right now, the countertops are littered with food containers, a mix of takeout and homemade. Pots and pans are stacked in the sink. There's a dishwasher left yawning open, partially full. And at a round table tucked beneath the window, we see Kazu and Kei are slumped in their chairs, each one gripping a microphone.

They aren't singing anymore. Kazu has his chair tipped back to a hazardous angle, dark hair piled on top of his head in a bun. He's thrown one muscled arm over his face. A few Sunshines lament that Apollo's eldest member isn't shirtless, but we shouldn't get too greedy. Does the skin-tight tank really count as a shirt? Come on.

Across from him, Kei has his head down on the table, swathed entirely in black. Less than twenty-four hours after this livestream, Apollo fashion accounts on Instagram will report that he's wearing a small fortune's worth of Givenchy. His sweater is a gorgeous, beautifully draped cashmere, and if we were able to tiptoe closer, we'd see that it's adorned with tufts of cat hair.

The cat himself is perched nearby. He swats at a portable karaoke machine with one paw. This regal beast has been christened Masamune, at least for now. Kei can't seem to settle on a name. He rotates between famous samurai and legendary swordsmiths, determined to find the moniker that rings true. Masamune might just stick, though. Sunshines will riot if it changes again.

Kazu brings his chair back down to the floor with a thud. The cat hops down and then into his lap. Bottles clink, and Namgyu murmurs, "Aww, there he is! Masamune-dono! Nyan, nyan! He's so cute, I wish he could live at the dorms with us. He loves Zuzu, see?"

"Keiichi," slurs Kazu, aiming his microphone at the cat, "the shogun should come back with us. Just do it. He shouldn't have to live in exile."

"No pets allowed," Kei slurs back at him. "I can follow the rules. And Masamune was a blacksmith, not a shogun." He sighs. "Idiot."

"Right, right. Forgot his name isn't Yoritomo anymore.

Yoritomo was last month." Kazu drops the microphone on the kitchen floor and makes no effort to reclaim it. He cuddles Masamune against his chest, sending three quarters of the livestream viewers into meltdown mode. Sunshines are enraptured, Sunshines are obsessed, Sunshines are wishing they'd been reincarnated as a cat.

Namgyu reads the comments and gasps. "Awww! Me too! I want to be a cat. Keiichi would take such good care of me. And I'd be dressed so nice all the time. What a life!" Then his face falls. "Oh, but then Max would sneeze every time I came near him. And he wouldn't want to be with me anymore. Oh, no. It's just too sad."

It's an unfortunate truth, but no one is listening to him. "What a good shogun," Kazu croons now, snuggling the cat as the chat log floods with mindless shrieking. "And you're good too, Keiichi. You're so good. Just... what a good kid. Don't you leave me, too. It's bad enough that Hwannie's leaving me."

Kei shifts in his seat, jostling bottles and the karaoke machine with his elbow and wincing at the racket that results. Without lifting his head, he points at Kazu, silver rings flashing. "You're the one leaving me. You can't live without Jaehwan-hyung, you'll go back to your family and abandon us. They'll give you some bullshit corporate job at Tachibana Group. Nepotism, that's what it is. Nepotism!"

"I won't leave you. I'll never leave you guys."

"You will." Kei makes an effort to sit up, but ultimately

fails. "I don't even know why we're bothering," he says. "We're all screwed without hyung. These are the end times. We'll never survive this, not with you in charge. You're useless, Kazuhiko."

Kazu nods, eyes closed, arms full of fluffy feline. "I am. It's true. I love you guys, though. Don't forget."

"Love isn't enough to keep us alive," Kei exclaims, sitting up now. He seizes the closest bottle to hand and brings it to his lips, head thrown back, draining it to the dregs. It's a water bottle, Namgyu informs us. He saw Ari put it there earlier. Meanwhile, Sunshines rapidly lose brain cells over the elegant line of Keiichi's neck. Never mind about reincarnating as a cat; let's come back as bottled beverages instead.

"Maybe it is," Kazu contradicts him. "Love could be enough! Nothing's stronger than love! My dad said that to me once!" He almost topples right out of the chair. Masamune abandons ship, darting under the table with an offended yowl.

"That," says Kei, brandishing the empty bottle at his eldest brother, "is the stupidest thing you've ever said to me. And you know what? I wish I could be like you. I wish I could be..." He sways a little in his seat, then puts his head down again, pillowed on the luxuriant fabric of his sweater. "I wish I could be... that stupid... I'd be so much happier..."

Kazu is almost yelling now. "Ya! You could never be stupid, Keiichi. You'll go higher than the rest of us. Just watch. I just know. Trust me."

The screen jumps. Namgyu's phone is taken away, and then Jaehwan's handsome face appears, along with his newly shorn hair. He smiles. "Sunshines. Are you here to see me off, too?"

This chat was already falling apart, but now it's deteriorating beyond repair. Sunshines greet him with endless rows of crying emoji and all-caps wailing, everyone distraught. Jaehwan scans the messages, Namgyu's cheek mashed against his. While the two in the kitchen continue with their circular argument, Jaehwan says, "This isn't goodbye. I'm going away on vacation for two years, and then I'll be back. Got it? No tears."

"Aww, but I'll definitely cry, leader-nim."

"Cry harder," says Jaehwan, ruffling Namgyu's hair. "Not Sunshines, though. They should never be crying." He leans in closer. "I'll always be here for you. I made a promise nine years ago. Take care of my members while I'm gone, okay? You know how they are."

He returns the phone to Namgyu, who films as Jaehwan slips past him into the kitchen. The arguing has tapered into despondent silence. We see Jaehwan reach out to tuck the tag back into the collar of Kei's sweater. "Come here, Gyu. Help me with Keiichi."

Namgyu bids farewell to Sunshines, requesting that they eat three meals a day and refrain from working too hard until the next time he sees them. Before he ends the livestream, he shows us one last glimpse of the kitchen, where Jaehwan is busy hauling Kazu to his feet. "Don't call me when you need a new liver," we hear him say, without heat. "What a mess, Kazuhiko."

"You should call me," Kazu replies. "You never call me."

"Yeah, I'll call you. I get fifteen minutes a week and you can have five. It won't take you long to tell me that you've lost half the kids and Nicky sold the rest at auction." Turning partway, Kazu's arm slung over his shoulders, Jaehwan shouts down the hall. "Ari-yah! Get your brother off that couch, it's time to go. Nami's downstairs with the van."

"I've got him, hyung."

Kazu wobbles on his feet. Masamune dashes past him with a meow. "That kid. He's so good. Ari's so easy to take care of. He should never leave me either."

Jaehwan maneuvers his stumbling cargo into the hallway, then comes to a dead halt. "Put that down," he hisses. Jesse's trademark wail reverberates through the apartment. Then Jaehwan's head snaps to the right. "*Don't* put that down," he tells Nicky, because who else would it be, "and see what happens."

"Take it easy on him, hyung. Ooh, and me too. I just thought it would be funny. And it is, right? It'll be funny soon. Just give it a second."

"It's starting," Kei moans. "This is it. This is all we get for the next two years. I hate it here."

All cheerfulness has drained out of Namgyu's voice.

"Two years is the longest time. It's just too long. Is it really time to go? I'm not ready. We love you, leader-nim. Aww, I already miss you so much."

"I love you guys too," Jaehwan replies, gently. "And I'll love you more when you're nowhere near me."

Code Orange

Eunjae

"**H**YUNG!!!!!!"

Eunjae careens out of the bathroom, half-dressed and completely confused. It's been a long day, the bulk of it spent in meetings and in front of cameras. He was about to take a quick shower. Now, who knows.

"Hyung, hyung, hyuuuuunnnnngggg!!!"

"ARI-HYUNG!!!!!!"

Younger brothers come piling in as soon as he unlocks the hotel room door. How are these three already tearing around, wild-eyed, still in the same outfits from that interview earlier? Did they even stop at their own rooms first? Apollo just arrived at this new place and Eunjae hasn't even gotten his bearings yet. At the very least, they could let him go through his hotel check-in routine of locating the nearest ice machine and figuring out which of the many pillows will be a viable option.

"Hyung! Hyuuuuunngggg!" Jesse starts shaking him. Kei throws the deadbolt and Max flops facedown onto the bed. Eunjae stops trying to comprehend what's happening and drags clingy Jesse to the bathroom, where he cuts the water in the shower and pulls his shirt back on. So much for that.

They emerge into total darkness. Kei has killed the lights for some reason. With the drapes drawn, the only pinprick of illumination comes from the glowing digits on the microwave.

Eunjae rakes a hand through his hair. He picks his way over to the bedside lamp and tugs on the chain. "What's going on?"

"What's going on?" Jesse explodes. "We're doomed, that's what's going on!"

Max huffs at this. "We? Don't you mean just you?"

"Jesse is doomed." Kei checks the locks again, then presses his back to the door like someone might come at it with a battering ram at any second. "And Max. Max is screwed too, but I didn't do anything. Can't the lights just stay off? Maybe the Captain will think nobody's in here."

"Why are you worried about that right now...?" Eunjae asks, although he's pretty sure that he doesn't want to know, or be involved, or perhaps end up implicated in whatever this is.

Max hurls a pillow at Kei. "What makes you think I'm screwed but you're not?"

Jesse curls up on Eunjae's previously pristine bed. He worms his way under the covers and emits a muffled wail. One arm breaks out, a finger pointing to the backpack they brought with them. "Just look," he tells Eunjae, in attitudes of despair. "See for yourself, hyung."

The other two have loud opinions about this proposed course of action. Kei is in favor of never opening the backpack again. Max thinks they should throw it into a canyon. He even goes so far as to start Googling the nearest available canyon while Jesse carries on wailing about certain doom.

Without waiting for them to come to an accord, Eunjae sits down with the backpack. Black leather, silver hardware, and a zipper tab stamped with MILANO, ITALY all scream that this belongs to Kei. That much is clear, but the rest is subject to conjecture. A chill comes over him. Again, does he even want to know?

He studies each of his brothers in turn, trying to get some clue as to what they've smuggled away this time. Because it's definitely a smuggling job; they behaved the same way after stealing Nicky's expensive Le Creuset stockpot. It was a limited edition color, the prized jewel of his collection. Nicky didn't boil them alive in that stockpot when it was returned, but by the end of his prolonged revenge campaign, they would've chosen that fate in a heartbeat.

Where have these three been tonight? Eunjae rewinds the evening in his head. They went to that interview, and everyone in the group was accounted for at dinner. Then Denny moved them to this new safehouse, a sleek hotel in the middle of downtown. It was chosen because there are executives from Emerald staying here as well. It makes the ongoing negotiations easier, cutting the amount of time spent languishing in traffic, but everyone was happier at the last place.

Anyway, the youngest three left with Denny after dinner. It was supposed to be Kei and Jesse, but then Max was bundled into the car as well. Kazu offered him a choice between going with Denny or getting drop-kicked into outer space. So, not really a choice. In Zu's defense, even the most laid back substitute leader has his limits. Max can't make a habit out of losing it on every reporter who asks about his 'whirlwind romance' with Hazel Lim. It's just too many fires to put out.

What on earth did they stuff into this backpack within the hour or so that they weren't at the hotel? Sighing, Eunjae yanks on the zipper and peers inside. Aaaaand then he zips it right back up again. "Oh, no. I want nothing to do with this." He shoves the thing at Jesse and points to the exit. "Out."

"But hyung," Jesse whines, "you don't understand!"

"You need to help us. We let you abuse your authority or some shit like that. I remember what you said, okay?"

Kei nods. "There's no way you could've gotten fired without us. Now you need to pay back the favor."

The younger ones almost never band together like this. It takes a situation where all of their lives are in jeopardy, and then they'll suddenly become sworn allies. "You too, then? Weren't you just saying this was Jesse's idea?"

"It was! I just happened to be standing there!"

"Liar! Keiichi is a liar!" Jesse yells in Japanese. "He wanted to read the plaque. He said that!" He pokes Max in the cheek. "Back me up, hyung. You're my only witness!"

"Here's what I witnessed: me, doing nothing wrong. I didn't even touch it. I was talking to Emma-noona while you guys were vandalizing the property."

Eunjae turns to Jesse. "Ahn Ji-woon. You did what?"

This triggers a renewed cycle of wailing. Jesse cowers behind Max, who keeps trying to duck behind Kei, who keeps trying to be shed of both and make a run for it.

"Waaaahh! Ari really just called me that, I must be dead, I think I'm bleeding out—"

"I fucking told you he's mean now! You thought I was lying?"

Jesse sniffles. "Not lying but like, exaggerating?"

"Ya. For the last time, what did you do?"

"Waaaah! This is going to give me nightmares!"

"We all wanted to look at it," Kei finally confirms, squeaking a bit.

Eunjae nods. "Good luck to all three of you."

"Hyung! Come on!"

A glance at the microwave shows that the time is now two minutes past nine. Eunjae's phone rings, just as it does most nights around now, and he answers it without even looking at the screen.

"Eunjae, what do you think?" asks Jiyeon. She never bothers with greetings, just goes straight to the matter at hand. "This cake or that cake? I sent a picture."

"I always forget that your phone has a camera..."

"Uh-huh. Very funny. Just go look, they're both on sale and I can't decide."

The other three are all ears. They peer over Eunjae's shoulder as if they, too, have been asked to weigh the merits of carrot cake over dulce de leche. Jesse goes a mile further and pounces on the phone.

"Noooonnnaaaa," he whines. "Emma-noona, can you come over? Like right now? Pleeeaasseee?"

Eunjae relieves him of the phone in one well-timed swoop. "Leave. And take that with you. I wasn't kidding when I said I want nothing to do with this. But you'll be hearing from me when I find out what really happened, that's a promise."

"Waaahhhhh—"

"Hyung, you can't be mad at me about this, I didn't do shit."

"Which baby brother is crying?" Jiyeon asks. "It seems serious."

"Jess. And the other two are here with him, but not for long." Eunjae takes a step toward Jesse, Max, and Kei. They back away warily but haven't given up just yet.

"Noona, please come over and help us! I mean, come over and help Ari-hyung feel better! He just misses you so much!" Jesse makes sure to bellow at the top of his lungs so that half of Los Angeles can hear every word. "Please, you have to come see him. He's so sad!" A bolt of inspiration strikes. In English, he tacks on, "Hyung feels *desolate*."

Kei decides to jump in. "It's pathetic. We can send you a

video." Why is he using such formal Korean?

"Emma-noona," ventures Max, "weren't you saying you felt like coming over anyway?"

"She's not coming over," Eunjae informs them, in no uncertain terms. "It's late and she worked at the shop all day so Denny could take care of us." To Jiyeon, he says, "I think you need both slices. And I'll call you back, okay? Ten minutes."

She laughs. "Eunjae, you don't want to see me?"

"Well, that's never been true."

"So can I come over, then?"

"No," says Eunjae. "Get some rest."

"Hmm. You sound like you mean it."

Now he's laughing, too. "I don't. You know that."

"You sounded so strict, though. I didn't even know you could sound like that." There's beeping in the background, and an electronic voice announcing prices. She's at the self-checkout, scanning grocery purchases. "It's cute. Do it some more."

Eunjae wonders if he'd feel less warm if he didn't have three brothers piled on top of him right now.

"I was planning to drive over there anyway," Jiyeon admits. "I'm pretty close by. Don't be mad, okay?"

"Noona, he'll be soooo mad. Then you can hear the scary voice again!"

"He'd only be mad for two seconds."

"That's a relief," she replies, "since I'm coming over."

The younger brothers congratulate one another heartily. Eunjae opens his mouth to protest, but it's hard to go through with it. His inclination is to hoard as much time with Jiyeon as he can, knowing that the weeks are numbered. The return flight to Seoul will soon be upon him.

He tries again. Otherwise, it will be on his conscience. "You're tired."

"And I've missed you all day. I'm coming over."

Eunjae locates the thermostat. He cranks it down from 75 to 68. "What about Denny?"

"What about him?"

"He said he has to secure the perimeter."

"Oh, that. I talked to him already. Put me on speaker, though? Just for a second."

He complies. The other three crowd around like it's a beacon in the wilderness. Then they tumble over themselves in shock when Jiyeon's voice comes through again.

"You took Denny's gong, didn't you?"

Kei squeaks again. Max has a hand clamped over his mouth, and Jesse's eyes are bulging out of their sockets. His contacts are sky blue. He only got away with this level of whimsy because Denny was too busy to notice when they left for the interview.

"WE DIDN'T MEAN TO WE JUST WANTED TO LOOK AT IT WE BARELY TOUCHED IT WE SWEAR!"

"He said not to touch it or there would be consequences," grumbles Max. "So then we kinda had to touch it."

"I never touched it," Kei maintains stoutly. "I would never betray the Captain like that."

"Uh-huh. But you took it, right? 'Cause it wasn't there when

I closed out the register tonight, and Jeannie says she last saw it before you three came with Denny to drop off groceries."

Eunjae heaves a protracted sigh. "Yeah, it's here."

"That's what I thought. This is a Code Orange, then. See you in… fifteen minutes. Maybe twenty. I'm not very far away but it looks like there's some traffic ahead."

"C-Code Orange?" stammers Jesse, when the call ends. "What's a Code Orange?"

"No idea," Eunjae replies. He's texting Jiyeon his room number and also an apology on behalf of his brothers, now about a paragraph long. If he hurries, he can still shower before she gets here. "Out," he orders his brothers, reversing into the bathroom. "Go get your keys from Zu, he's in 407. The rest of your luggage is there too. You can grab those and be back in thirty, easy."

"Hey, Emma-noona said she'd be here in twenty," says Max, eyes narrowed.

"But I'm getting so sleepy," Jesse complains. "I'm emotionally drained."

"I'm not going to Grandpa's room. He stops wearing clothes after 8pm."

"That's what I'm saying, Keiichi. I'm too emotionally drained for this. Like I just don't have the bandwidth."

Eunjae uses his phone to take a picture of the backpack. "Alright. I'll just let Denny know what you've got in there. You can wait for him here if you want."

And suddenly he's alone in his room, the incriminating backpack abandoned on the bed. He doesn't appreciate being saddled with the evidence, but Eunjae figures it's best for the gong to stay right where it is. Who knows what else could happen to it in the meantime?

Not quite twenty minutes later, Jiyeon shows up with both cake slices, a fruit tray, and a gallon of orange juice. She's still wearing her Wanna Waffle t-shirt, tie-dyed by Jeannie last summer. All the colors are blurred, filtered in soft focus after being through the wash so many times. It reminds Eunjae of those evenings at the Hans' apartment, waiting for her knock at the door, for the best part of his day to begin. She's still the best part of his day. But now he can kiss her when she comes by after work, and they are currently not surrounded by brothers, so he doesn't have to worry about who might catch them.

Life is pretty good.

"Busy day?"

"Gosh, yeah. I'm glad we have Jeannie and Evan full time until the end of July." She pops the lid off the fruit tray and spears some cantaloupe with a plastic fork. "Denny said I could come if I promised to quit bringing 'snacks of questionable nutritional value' when I see you."

"I'll pretend I didn't see any cake."

"Just help me come up with a good apology when he asks." She holds out the fork. "Here. Then I can say I'm in compliance."

Eunjae leans down and obediently allows himself to be fed. He's still chewing when Jesse, Max, and Kei announce their arrival by pounding on the door like Viking invaders. He thinks about making them wait out there for another five minutes. No, ten.

That wouldn't kill them, right? But they're so noisy, and what if the commotion brings Denny up here? Until the gong situation is sorted out, Eunjae would rather avoid that outcome. So he opens the door, with marked reluctance, and they all run right past him to throw themselves at Jiyeon... exactly like he knew they would.

Life is pretty good, but also he has too many brothers.

"Emma-noona! We just saw you but I think you got prettier!"

"Are you saying that 'cause you want candy? I only have a fruit tray today." She gestures at Kei. "I was told you're looking 'peaky' so the orange juice is for you. Eunjae put it in the mini fridge if you want to take it back to your room later."

"I do feel peaky," says Kei, awestruck. He heads to the fridge and grabs the orange juice, treating it with great reverence.

"It's even that snobby brand you like so much, Your Highness. Denny thinks of everything!"

Max was the first to get himself a fork from the package in the grocery bag. He's cleared out all the strawberries in the fruit tray and has now moved on to the pineapple. "Denny's the best manager we've ever had," he says.

"He's... the *king* of managers."

"And if he finds out what we did," says Kei, returning with a glass wrapped in hotel-branded tissue paper, "he'll leave us." He pours himself a glass of orange juice, looking grim.

"You've gotta help! What do we do? We didn't mean to break it."

Eunjae swallows a mouthful of watermelon, mostly unchewed. Appalled, he chokes out, "You broke it?"

"By accident!"

"Keiichi doesn't know his own strength."

"Jesse's the one who rang the gong, not me!"

"But you were holding it," Max reasons, "so maybe it was your fault that it broke."

"You idiots always gang up on me!"

As the accusations fly, Jiyeon leans against Eunjae, trying very hard not to laugh. He slings an arm around her, frowning at his brothers. "That gong is really important to him. It's an award. He won it last year."

"From the Lemon Grove Asian American Business Association," adds Jiyeon. "Mom's the one who accepted the award at the banquet, since the shop is under her name, but we all know it belongs to Denny. It's for building such a strong community at Wanna Waffle. You can only be nominated by members of the community, and then it's decided by a judging panel and a popular vote."

"I would've known that," murmurs Jesse, lip wobbling, "if Keiichi hadn't broken the gong before I could read the plaque. And now it's too late! Noona, I'm *aggrieved*."

"I didn't break it! Shut up!"

Max steals a swig of orange juice directly from the gallon jug. "You guys really fucked up. Denny's never coming to Seoul with us now."

"You want him to come with you?" asks Jiyeon.

As one, Eunjae's younger brothers shout, "Yes!"

"We talked about this," he replies. "Denny has a job here.

He runs the shop seven days a week. We can't hire him to be our manager. He's done so much as it is, and he'll probably stay with us until it's time to go, so we can't ask anything more from him."

"But we need Denny," Kei insists. "Hyung, if we lose the Captain, we go back to living in chaos. And when we finish up all the stuff we have left on contract for Emerald, we won't have a manager, period. Not until we sign with another agency."

Jesse nods. "Wherever we go, we need Denny. We'll die without him. I'm not ready to do that, hyung. I need more time. I've barely even been alive yet."

"Murder-hyung's not out for another year and a half. Zu can't go it alone that whole time." Max chugs some more orange juice, either not noticing or not caring that Kei is staring daggers at him the whole time, and for more than one transgression. "What a deadbeat dad."

"The worst!"

"It must be tough for Kazu," says Jiyeon. "Eunjae ran away, and then Max stole Jungwoo's girlfriend…"

The accused girlfriend thief turns around, mouth hanging open. "Noona, goddamn!"

"But isn't that what you did? Sure, Jungwoo said they weren't really together anymore, but it's not like you knew. And it's not okay just because they were already on the rocks when it happened."

"Hazel was supposed to—"

"Deny it," she cuts in, finishing the sentence for him. "And then she didn't, plus she's telling the press it was love at first sight.

For you, not for her." Jiyeon replaces the lid on what is now an empty fruit tray. "I think it serves you right."

Max rounds on Eunjae. "I thought she was my friend!"

"I am your friend," says Jiyeon, "and also... I think it serves you right."

By this point, Jesse and Kei are on the floor, having laughed themselves right off the furniture. Kei regains enough composure to say, "Ari-hyung, talk to the Captain for us. He's basically your brother-in-law thanks to pure dumb luck. He'll listen to you."

"That's right!" Jesse cries out. "Noona, when you marry our worthless brother, can I have my own room in your house?"

Max glowers at him. "Worthless? She could've done way worse. Ari's not stupid-rich like Zuzu, but I bet he has a savings account, at least."

"Another plus," says Jiyeon.

Jesse takes over most of the bed, chin propped up in his hands. "But what do you even like about hyung? I wanna know."

"It's a long list. Ask me when we have more time."

"Okay, stay on topic," Eunjae interrupts. Maybe he should've dropped the thermostat all the way down to 60. 50. Subarctic temperatures. "Let's see if we can fix the gong and put it back without Denny finding out what you did. That's the most important thing right now."

"Will you talk to him, though? About coming with us? Pleeeeaaasseeee."

He starts to tell them no for the umpteenth time, but then Jiyeon says, "I think Denny likes being your manager. Actually, I've been thinking… that he enjoys managing you a lot more than he enjoys managing the shop."

Eunjae catches her eye. "You really think so?"

"Uh-huh. You keep him so busy. I mean, running a restaurant does too, and Denny loves Wanna Waffle. He's loved the place since he was a kid. But I do feel like he needed a change of pace, even if he wouldn't admit it. He's sort of mastered being a restaurant manager to the point that there's not much challenge left anymore."

"We are pretty challenging," admits Eunjae, with a sigh. Kei sighs along with him in wordless agreement.

"And also, you're fun." Jiyeon smiles. "He doesn't show it very well, but Denny's happy to be with you. Happy to have so many brothers." She holds up a hand. "Don't tell him I said all that. And don't tell him Mom and Jeannie said the same thing while we were closing up."

Kei's mood takes an abrupt upswing. "The Captain likes us!"

"I think he only likes Ari-hyung. Calm down."

"If Emma-noona tells hyung to do it," Jesse whispers in Kei's ear, "he'll go ask Denny right now. Watch."

"It's not a bad idea. I can keep covering while he's gone. I don't have a new job lined up yet, anyway." Jiyeon glances at Eunjae. "I know what you're about to say, but it really is fine. Denny should get to do this if he wants to. You agree, don't you?"

Eunjae does agree. And he does want Denny to come, just like everyone else. He keeps things running so smoothly that it's kind of eerie sometimes, but his presence has also felt like a bulwark against the great unknown. Denny has a way of reducing the most insurmountable prospects into piles of pebbles on the shore. There is no problem that can't be solved. There is no obscure task, service, or request that can't be completed with effective use of resources.

Denny strikes fear into Eunjae's heart. At the same time, Denny is a comfort. Denny is part of home.

But then there's Jiyeon, who always says she'll be fine. What if she won't be? How will she get a new salon off the ground while also juggling the shop during these months without Denny? She wouldn't have time to do her own thing.

They'll be gone at least until September, maybe longer. Eunjae is determined to cut it shorter if he can, but there are no guarantees. It feels like negotiations with Emerald will never end, now that the new plan involves finishing out the group's existing obligations. Just about the only thing he can say with certainty is that he's asking Jiyeon to put up with so much. It only gets worse when he reflects on how much he's asked of the Hans as a whole. It's hard to imagine a day when he'll be clear of all the debts he owes them.

"Eunjae."

"Mm."

"Why don't we just talk to Denny about it? He's the one who should decide, anyway. If you offer this, it'll be his choice to make."

She squeezes his hand. Eunjae gives up. "We'll ask him," he tells his brothers.

Gasps all around. Kei looks like he might erupt into song and dance. Jesse starts jumping on the bed, propelling himself higher and higher. Max just grins. He hasn't grinned that way in a while. It takes forever to restore a semblance of calm, but Eunjae is glad to see them showing so much appreciation for Denny. It's deserved.

Then he has to explain, very firmly, that the whole group is responsible for making sure they write up a fair agreement, something more concrete than the one they have now. "Denny should be paid what he's worth, too. That means everybody chips in, because he wouldn't be on Emerald's payroll. He'd be on ours."

"I have money," says Kei, affronted.

"International Bank of Kazuhiko!"

"Everyone's paying him, Jess. Not just Zu. And that's only if Denny wants to come. If he doesn't, you drop it. No whining."

Another gasp. "I would never whine about it."

"All three of you need to agree right now. I need to hear you say it."

"Waaahh, we already have Jaehwan-hyung with the terms and conditions, we don't need more terms and conditions!"

Eunjae just waits. Soon enough, they agree not to whine, but in decidedly whiny tones. "See?" grumbles Max. "What did I tell you?"

"Sooooo mean," whimpers Jesse.

Jiyeon taps Kei on the shoulder, asking if she can see the gong. The backpack is produced and its contents lifted out for inspection. "So it broke in the same spot," she muses, gingerly fitting the fragments together. "See? This is where we fixed it during the last Code Orange. It was Dad's fault that time."

"What happened?" asks Max. But then there's a whirring sound from the lock mechanism on Eunjae's door, and Jiyeon stuffs the gong back into the bag, shunting it under the bed.

Bells should ring whenever Denny enters a room. Eunjae's always thought so. Gigantic, booming bells that toll expressly for the damned.

"Captain!" bleats Kei. "Good evening! We aren't doing anything suspicious, Captain!"

"Stand down, Moriyama." Denny tosses his sizable overnight bag onto the bed like it's nothing but a sack stuffed with feathers. He glares at the younger brothers. They freeze in place, reminding Eunjae of rabbits listening for the telltale sibilance of a snake. "What are you three doing here?"

"Nothing!"

"Drinking orange juice! For my health!"

"They heard the cantaloupe was good," says Jiyeon, mouth twitching at the corners. "What a nutritious snack. Right, Eunjae?"

"Ah, yeah. That's it."

"Hmph," Denny grunts. "Acceptable. They're starting to look jaundiced. Go to bed! Your corporate overlords want to meet over breakfast."

The younger brothers flee the scene, only pausing so Jesse can hiss, "Remember, hyung! Ask him! Ask him tonight!"

Denny has already shifted his focus to Jiyeon. "You need to go too, Yeonnie. 5am gets here faster than you think."

She nudges the backpack a little further under the bed. "You get to stay with Eunjae and I don't?"

"You can stay if you want. You're the one losing sleep. It's your funeral."

"But you'll be here too?"

"Ryan Kim," Denny intones, "is a blessed innocent. He needs a chaperone."

"A blessed innocent."

"Don't play dumb, Han Jiyeon!"

"I'm not playing dumb, I know exactly what you're saying. And if you're so concerned about Eunjae's innocence, why don't you go bunk with someone else and I'll fix that for him—"

"Right, so we're done talking about that now," says Eunjae, somehow, from the brink of a nervous meltdown. He pulls up a chair and invites Denny to sit. Then he maneuvers Jiyeon to the extreme opposite side of the bed, very far away from his own spot, for personal survival purposes. Once everyone is situated in a manner which compromises no virtues and triggers no chaperoning impulses, he throws himself wholeheartedly into changing the subject.

"Boss, we were wondering. Would you consider staying on as our manager?"

Denny stares at him. "What, like officially?"

"Yeah. You'd have to come with us to Seoul for a few months, and I know what you'd be leaving behind. But if you're willing, we'd make sure it was worth your time and effort. You'd work for us, not the agency, and not any agency we might sign with in the future."

"But why?" It's the first time Eunjae has ever seen Denny so mystified. "I don't even have any prior experience. Shouldn't you go with someone who has relevant credentials?" Denny frowns. "Ryan, you guys really need to evaluate your hiring practices."

Jiyeon gets up and relocates so that she's sitting right next to Eunjae, thereby jeopardizing his status as a blessed innocent. "Hmm. Maybe they just like you, Den."

"We do. We all want you to stay with us. And I think everybody just wants someone we can trust, after everything that happened."

"Everybody...? All ninety of you said that...?"

"It's unanimous. But it's okay if you don't want to. We understand that we're, uh, a lot to handle."

"No joke. You're a bunch of toddlers carrying glitter in salt shakers."

"Ah, yeah."

"A circus train," says Denny, settling into his chair, "pulling eight cars packed with clown costumes and high-grade explosives."

Eunjae sighs. "Pretty much."

"Downhill track," he goes on. "Sixty degree incline. The brakes are shot and agents of the opposition government have tampered with the rails."

Jiyeon shakes her head. "Denny. Come on."

"What? He just offered me a job managing some feral kittens full time. I'm allowed to request clarification on the role." But his expression grows thoughtful. "Feral kittens who speak a minimum of three languages apiece.... easily crossing international borders...

providing musical entertainment to the masses, that's a built-in cover. Huh."

"Um. Yes?"

"There's potential. If we threw in some guerrilla warfare drills..."

"Do you want to go with them or not?" Jiyeon asks, nudging Denny's knee with her foot. "I think you do. And we want you to go, okay? We can run the shop for a few months without you. Don't let that be your excuse."

There's a significant pause before Denny responds, fuming. "You guys just don't want me around anymore. Is that it?"

"Not even close. We'll miss you, honestly. No one's even mentioned it to Dad in case he gets too emotional. It'll be rough, but we'll be fine. This would be a great opportunity for you. And it's not just 'cause you're good at it, being their manager."

"But you really are good at it," adds Eunjae. "We've never had better."

Jiyeon smiles. "Go 'cause it makes you happy, Denny."

Now the pause stretches out, possibly to infinity, and Eunjae worries that this is too much pressure with too little notice. "Don't rush. It's just that we have to arrange a working visa and all this other stuff. I looked it up the other night."

"Visa's not an issue," Denny scoffs. "That's all I can say. It's classified."

Jiyeon snorts at this. Denny snorts back at her, then looks over at Eunjae. "What's the benefits package?"

"The best we can manage." Eunjae hasn't gotten that far, but he'll figure it out.

"Vacation days?"

"Sick days too."

"Trick question. I've only been sick two times," declares Denny, "and vacations are a scam."

"Our Woosung," his sister says, rolling her eyes. But she's still smiling, and Denny extends a colossal hand in Eunjae's direction. His eyes are shining.

"Ryan," he booms out. "I accept the mission."

Eunjae leaps up and gives Denny's hand a firm shake. It's not unlike shaking hands with the marble effigy of a titan. Cross that experience off the list.

"You're hired, then." He makes sure the backpack containing the gong has been pushed so far under the bed that there's no way Denny will see it. "And, uh, please don't kill us."

That will have to be the first line in the contract.

Inside the dining room at Wanna Waffle, the shades are drawn and the tables scrubbed clean. Evan has mopped every inch of the floor except for one corner near the back, headphones on, humming to himself. He stayed late again tonight. Although it's been a while since the shop closed for the day, there's been so much to do.

The person responsible for this unusual level of after-hours activity is a pop star named Kazu who also happens to be a millionaire's nephew. He stands in the middle of the room, evaluating what his money has purchased. His own money, mind you. Or what's left of it, considering how often Kazu loses to Jaehwan in a bet.

"Looking good," he announces, pleased. "Seems like they match the blue you had on the old ones."

"You spent so much money," chides Mrs. Han. "You didn't need to replace every chair!" But she has to dab at her eyes with the handkerchief Kei loaned her five minutes ago — Prada, silk, dry clean only — and when Jungwoo pauses to offer her a seat, she can't stop smiling.

"I'm doing the booths, too. Still waiting on some quotes." In response to this, we hear someone loudly remarking that their dad is sooooo super rich and he'll spend aaaallll that money on literally anybody other than his kids. Kazu threatens wind sprints and the remarks fizzle out into resentful silence.

"It's too much. You are a very sweet boy, Kazuhiko. I have to write your mommy and daddy a letter, tell them all about you."

Kazu decides to try out a chair as well. He says, "They'd be mad if I didn't do anything for you. Don't worry about it. This is a gift, for taking care of Ari."

"You know, that kid he lost?" Max contributes as he passes by. He's got one of the old chairs tucked under his arm, off to stack it with the rest outside. There's a waffle in his free hand. It's been skewered on a fork like a giant lollipop. Taking a bite, he adds, "Deadbeat dad."

"The worst!"

"What? We found him eventually."

On the other side of the room, Mr. Han watches as Namgyu decimates Jesse in another round of tic-tac-toe. And in the adjacent booth, Denny and Jiyeon glare at each other, backs straight and arms crossed. Never have they looked so much like siblings. It's total war. It's pistols at dawn.

"And what I'm telling you," we hear Denny arguing, "is that if I did, theoretically, use Ryan as bait in a mission-critical situation—"

"I don't understand why he would even be with you in a mission-critical situation. What mission-critical situation? Why would that ever need to happen?"

"In dire circumstances."

"That doesn't mean anything to me," Jiyeon replies flatly. She twists the cap onto a plastic water bottle and sets it down on the table, hard.

Jesse lets out a wail. "I'll never beat hyung, I give up! This isn't even fun, it's just sad, it's *demoralizing*—"

"Aww, it's true that you can't beat me. I love you though, Jess. I love you so much!"

"If you loved me," Jesse whines, "you'd let me win sometimes. But whatever! Let's just have the Captain watch another video instead."

Neither the Captain nor his sister catches what he said. "I think Eunjae should just stay with me," Jiyeon maintains.

"You can go on any mission-critical-whatever that you feel like doing, though. It's your life."

Eunjae walks up just then, dressed in a hodgepodge of garments that don't match in the slightest but still work, somehow: his Wanna Waffle t-shirt, some random shorts, a billowing gray cardigan with elbow patches and a four-figure price tag. We see him stopping to say goodbye to Mr. and Mrs. Han, who are heading home. Then Eunjae dries his hands on a dish towel, putting his glasses back on. "Ah, where am I going?"

She gestures at the spot beside her. "Right here," she answers, glaring at Denny, "and nowhere else."

"Well, that's easy," says Eunjae. He slides into the booth, dish towel thrown over one shoulder. "Wanted to be there anyway."

"She isn't comprehending the scope of the mission, Ryan. Just because you'd be the bait, doesn't mean you'd end up in the direct line of fire for longer than five, six seconds. Six point five, tops. I'd get you out of there with minimal damage. In, out, home for dinner."

Jiyeon leans forward. "Excuse me?"

"Caaapptttaaaiiinnnnnn," Jesse wails now, blond head peeking over the plexiglass divider between his booth and theirs. Once again, he's roped an irritated Kei into pointing a phone at Denny's face. "Look up there! Look at the TV! It's time to watch another video!"

U SHINE (2014)

A golden coin flashes into being, spinning slowly on the screen. It's stamped with a stylized sun on one side and a logo on the reverse. As the coin spins slower and slower, we see the letter A radiating beams of light. It's Apollo's logo, and this is their debut music video. It premiered on February 20, 2014.

As if compelled by some powerful gravitational force, the coin plunges through space. Stars and galaxies rush past in a blur. And then the coin hits a dark, polished floor. It spins a few times, and just before it's about to fall flat, a hand reaches down to pick it up.

[PAUSE]

"Oh, no," says Jungwoo. "Does it have to be this one?"

"Haha... aww, man..." Namgyu pinches Jesse's cheek. "I gotta go, baby brother. Auntie and Uncle can give me a ride. Love you so much! Bye!"

"That's so dramatic, hyung! We all looked like garbage in this video, it wasn't just you—"

"Ya, you can't all stay here," says Kazu, on the verge of leaving as well. "Keiichi, you ride with us too."

Jesse pouts. "He can't leave! Hyung's helping me! Some of us can ride with the Captain. Ari's riding with

Emma-noona, anyway. We all know he is. And Max will try to go with them because he wants to be a third wheel when he grows up."

"You should take Nicky," Kei calls out. "Do you even know where he is?"

Eunjae glances at Jiyeon, then glances away again. She watches him for a moment, puzzled. "What's up? Why do you look so nervous?"

"Nothing," he replies. "It's nothing." Then he adds, "Don't be mad."

"Mad about what...?"

The golden coin is pushed through a slot, activating a pinball machine that floats all by itself in outer space. The camera pans until we're looking at—

[PAUSE]

Denny vacates his side of the booth, then makes a beeline for the kitchen. "Stand by, Moriyama."

"Captain! Yes, Captain!"

Kei pauses the video. Everyone waits until Denny returns, marching Nicky in front of him like an inmate at a maximum security prison. Is that waffle batter on his shirt? What he's been up to this whole time, we'll never know. But

Nicky takes captivity in stride, as usual, and he becomes exponentially more gleeful when he sees what's on the screen.

"Oooooh," he says, as Denny equips him with an embroidery hoop and a cross stitch pattern that will take weeks to complete. "Guys, this was a great choice. Who hasn't seen it yet? You, ajumma? Because let me just say... what a treat."

"Hmm. No, I haven't seen it yet."

"Perfect. That's just perfect." Nicky makes himself nice and comfortable in the booth. He nods at Eunjae. "I'm sure you'll still think he's hot after you see this. Don't worry."

"Ah, hyung..."

"Ah, hyung..." Jiyeon finishes for him. "I'm just some guy from Brisbane."

Eunjae laughs. "Is that what I sound like?"

"Oh, that was very nice. I didn't know you had this talent, ajumma. Here, do me next."

Jiyeon frowns a little in contemplation. Then she takes her water bottle, removes the cap, and tosses the remaining inch of water into Nicky's face. With a grin, she says, "But wasn't that so funny?"

The performance earns her multiple rounds of applause. From Nicky, she gets a standing ovation.

The camera pans until we're looking at Apollo's leader, Jaehwan! There's a pendant dangling from the thick gold chain *around his neck, stamped with the word FAMOU$. The letters have been spelled with a mix of emeralds and diamonds. Yes, the S is a dollar sign. This bejeweled atrocity swings back and forth as he pushes a heart-shaped button, starting the game. The game, by the way, is this room. It's the whole universe. We were in a game all along! Pixels cascade onto the screen, invoking retro titles that were considered vintage long before anyone in Apollo would've been old enough to play.*

Jaehwan sings the opening lines, smirking at the viewer. His eyeliner is so bold that it's natural to wonder if the poor boy showed up on set with a matching pair of shiners. But it's the hair that will surely stun you into paying attention. What a vivid shade of yellow! And it's been gelled into a ring of spikes around his head, like the halo of a crazed saint—

[PAUSE]

The dining room is in an uproar. Kei defends their leader's honor. Jesse is clinging to Kei and laughing, but the worst of the noise comes from Kazu. He's all set to laugh himself into a stupor. No one can get anything coherent out of him. In the end, Namgyu comes back to pull him outside, eyes carefully averted from the screen.

As if to balance out the saintliness, here's Jesse with his hair twisted into adorable little devil horns! He's kitted out in black from head to toe, from the shredded jean jacket to the even more bedraggled shorts. Since his hair is also an inky black, the effect is of a rain cloud with legs, hopping from one animated platform to the next. But one platform disintegrates beneath him, and then Jesse is tumbling through space—

"I almost forgot that Emerald was trying to sell Jess as the bad one, in the beginning," muses Jungwoo.

"Oh my goosssshhhh, it's so funny, it's the funniest thing ever because Max is the bad one."

Denny finally speaks. "How old were you when they did this, Ahn?"

Apollo begins debating the age of their youngest member at debut. It's starting to look like they'll need to Google their own maknae when Denny grunts, "Regardless, this has to be a violation of child labor laws. That amount of hair gel is a health hazard and a fire hazard at the same time. And the emotional damage they caused by making you look like the saddest member of Cirque du Soleil—"

The choreography for U SHINE *is an ambitious and totally deranged cardio workout from hell. Nicky takes the point position as main dancer, and you can't let yourself be fooled by his effortless delivery. In the years after Apollo debuted, Emerald Entertainment trainees have joked that being made to dance this choreo is a form of torture. At least, that's what they say until a variety show puts them through the industry-wide hazing ritual that is Apollo's* Break Point *at 2x speed.*

Anyway, dear Sunshines, what I'm trying to tell you is that Nicky is moving too fast — and the camerawork is too manic — to get a good handle on what he's wearing. For now, we'll need to be content with a flash of hot pink hair and these sneakers all the members are wearing for the dance shots. They have thick rubber light-up soles like this is fifth grade in 1995.

[PAUSE]

Max strolls in from outside, his waffle long gone. The group is in chaos. Half are complaining about the lasting trauma caused by this choreography. The other half demands accountability for Nicky's crimes, citing the fact that they will never be free of this choreo until they retire or die, whichever comes first.

"We'll be dead because it'll kill us," Kei pronounces gravely.

"No shit. *U Shine* is on every set list."

"And when *Break Point* comes after it..." Eunjae's shoulders sag. "Remembering makes me tired."

Jesse starts throwing boba straws at Apollo's choreographer. "When will you go to jail, hyung? Just go, like just put yourself in there, you're worse than Zuzu—"

"Hey, I put us on the map, okay? We had to stand out. Nobody even knew who we were." Nicky grins. "And now they'll never forget. That's thanks to me, okay? None of you pulled out a scandal until literally 2023. I had to do all this work by myself."

He waves the embroidery hoop at Denny. "Can you believe that, Chief? They have no gratitude. I made them famous, and all the little Emerald trainees have to dance our debut song for their monthly evals because of the supreme technical difficulty."

Denny dismisses him with a wave. "Talk to me when you can dance and throw knives at the same time, Kim Ahnjong. Lee's girlfriend, the actress? She did it in that movie, the one where she's an assassin. Heard she does most of her own stunts. Why you guys aren't asking for lessons is beyond me. That's a resource and you're just squandering it."

"Oooh, why *are* we squandering this resource, Max? Why don't you share your *resource* with us? Or do we have to steal her, maybe the Chief here is interested—"

"He's married to the business!" snaps Kei.

As for Max, he takes an entire fistful of straws and launches them at Nicky. "You can fuck right off, hyung. And if Denny wants Hazel, he can have her. I'll even pay him, she never shuts up—"

"Can we just keep watching?" sighs Jungwoo.

Now we're in an actual arcade. The scene is lit by a soft neon glow; an aurora of undulating pixels has been projected onto the walls. But who is this, delivering the pre-chorus as he leans against a claw machine? Oh wow, that's Ari! The stylists have assigned him a black tee with a screen-printed bow tie at the collar. Suspenders hold up ripped jeans with bedazzled patches at both knees. His hair is about jaw-length, ocean blue, and crimped within an inch of its life—

[PAUSE]

We've plummeted into a maelstrom of noise. The victim of this fashion nightmare is slowly melting out of the booth and onto the floor, covering his face with both hands.

"Ryan," Denny roars at him. "You didn't fight? You just let them do this to you?" He stands, bracing himself against the table in order to interrogate Eunjae even as the latter continues to expire from embarrassment. "Look, I get that you're lacking in proper martial arts training, but you could at least scream for help. Threaten to sue."

"I've always said he could punch them and run," says Max, a man who is always full of helpful suggestions. He's crouched on the floor, picking up the mess of boba straws. "Fall down and play dead. Or just tell the stylists to fuck off.

Keiichi does it all the time."

"Ohmygoshohmygoshohmygooossshhh. The time they tried to put Keiichi-hyung in the one outfit with the stretchy black shirt-thing, I was so scared, I thought I was about to witness three murders and I'd have to testify against my own brother in court—"

"It was polyester or something," says Jungwoo. "Or viscose."

Kei tosses his head, eyes closed. "I'll die first."

"How dare they attempt to clothe His Royal Highness the dark mage Adrianos in anything less than the finest fabrics of the Lunar Fells? You will know my vengeance—"

"ADRIAZOS!"

As this conversation devolves into a marathon of dark prince impersonations, Denny crouches next to the booth, addressing Eunjae under the table. "For god's sake, Ryan. They dressed you like an assistant professor at a community college. And the college is in a cartoon. And the cartoon only airs on Thursdays at 3am because no kid with self-respect is ever watching it voluntarily. What's next? A bunch of talking bears? Bumblebees singing show tunes? I've never seen anything goofier in my life. This is why I keep saying you need combat training."

But the real focus should be on Jiyeon, who has bravely endured a parade of hairstyling crimes up until now. While her brother continues ranting, she hauls Eunjae into a seated position. Taking his face into her hands, she says, "I can't watch this." Then Jiyeon evacuates to the kitchen.

Eunjae goes after her. "Ari-hyung!" Jesse calls after him, giggling. "Dad said you have to leave the door open from now on! Don't forget!"

And here is Nicky again, hitting us with rap lines this time. The camera zooms in. Now we can see that his long bangs have been slicked diagonally across his face. Imagine an eyepatch, but it's your own hair. He winks at us. How charming!

[PAUSE]

"Hey, I practiced that wink. You know how hard it was to wink with my other eye instead?"

Kei skips the video forward, grimacing. "You want a medal for it or something? Weirdo."

"It's creepy as fuck, hyung," Max concurs.

"Waaahhh, gives me soooo many nightmares, just imagine if you found that at the foot of your bed at like two in the morning..."

"This group," says Nicky, shaking an embroidery needle at him, "has the most disrespectful maknae line in the whole industry. It's tragic that none of my sons can appreciate artistry."

Max and Jungwoo appear next. As neon hearts race across the floor, they slouch against the wall with their arms around one another's shoulders. Those acid wash jeans are at least ten years behind the initial trend and another ten years away from enjoying an inevitable, cursed resurgence. Max's hair has been teased into a pompadour, then bleached such a brilliant shade of white that it leaves you feeling snow-blind.

As for Jungwoo, the hairstyle seems tame enough, if dated. But then the camera swings around, revealing that the entire left side has been shaved, and someone airbrushed a lightning bolt onto his scalp—

[PAUSE]

"Artistry!" squeals Jesse.

"I forgot they were trying to sell Max and Jungwoo as a duo. I'll never figure out why."

"They were supposed to be the bestest, best best friends."

"GROSS!"

Denny is on his feet again. He points at Jungwoo. "Press charges. It's not too late."

"Press charges?" Jungwoo sits up. "Against Max? I mean, it sucks that he did that to me, but it's not against the law."

The others crack up. Max glowers at his older brother,

turning a very nice shade of red. "The hell would you even charge me with? And by the way, she asked you to speak up and you didn't!"

"How could I say anything? Haven't we been over this?"

"You weren't saying anything because she doesn't fucking mean anything to you anyway—"

"Now, my sons. Hear me out." Nicky tries to get out of the booth, but can't wheedle his way past the immovable crag that is Denny. He perches on top of the table instead.

"Listen to this. Just listen. We could settle everything once and for all. Jungwoo challenges Max to a duel, then we televise it. Merch, VIP tickets, the works. I take a 40% cut for expenses and being a genius. We donate the other 60% to charity, and BOOM. PR issue resolved." It's like we can see a lightbulb turning on above his head. "Oooh, plus we bring Hazel on stage. Loser gets socked in the jaw."

Denny seizes him by the collar of his shirt, yanking him backwards and onto the bench. "Kim Ahnjong."

"I know! It's so funny, right?"

We encounter Ari again for the bridge, but then the focus shifts to Namgyu during the final chorus. Like Jesse, he's dressed in black. Have you ever seen such a severe bowl cut in your life? And don't look now, but that might be his natural hair color, last seen in 2014. This phenomenon might never occur again during our lifetimes.

Jesse hoots at the TV. "I almost didn't recognize him,"

he exclaims. "It doesn't even look like Gyu. Gosh, can we leave Emerald a second time? Can we just quit again? This counts as career sabotage, right?"

"But we skipped Kei," says Jungwoo. "Didn't we? I thought he was after Gyu but right before Kazu-hyung..."

Kei shoots him a withering glare. He has a death grip on the remote and refuses to rewind to his part of the video.

"Oh my gosh, Captain. Like, you just really need to see it sometime. Keiichi's hair was longer, they were trying to make him a Kazu clone or something, Kazu Junior—"

"Shut up!"

"And they put these glittery beads in his hair, too," Jesse crows. "That was the other time I thought Kei might kill someone on set. Except we were brand new, right, so he couldn't be such a diva yet."

"Glittery beads..." Denny digs the car keys out of his pocket. "My condolences, Moriyama. You can take shotgun on the drive home."

"Captain!" Kei exclaims. "I would even just ride on the roof, Captain!"

The video closes with none other than Kazu. The shirt is black mesh and those are... some extremely low-rise jeans. He tosses that dark, lustrous mane out of his face—

[PAUSE]

"Wait. Why doesn't Ueda look any different?"

"Because Zuzu's a diva too, actually."

Jungwoo nods. "Yeah, he's never changed his hair this whole time. Not the color or the style or anything. Except when he's grown it out longer."

This is when Eunjae pops up in the kitchen doorway, Jiyeon right behind him. "Ah, it's time to go home, right? Anyone riding with us?" As predicted, Max tears across the room to join him. After much deliberation from the Captain, Nicky is allowed to go as well. This leaves Kei, Jungwoo, and Jesse to watch the last scene in the video with Denny.

The group gathers for an ending pose, slipping into their assigned spots with perfect synchrony. Kazu flicks a golden coin into the air. We follow as it ascends into what is presumably the stratosphere, and then outer space, in open defiance of both physics and gravity. The coin spins slowly until Apollo's logo is in view. Then, the screen blinks out.

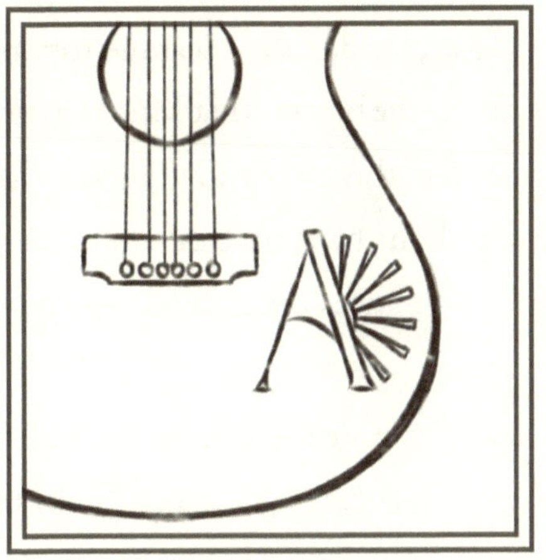

Not Asking Much

Jiyeon

THE VERY LAST SAFEHOUSE is a modern monstrosity, all concrete and metal and glass. Straight lines fold into sharp corners. During the day, looking at the place makes Jiyeon's eyes feel bruised. But right now, under the stars, it isn't so bad. The long reflecting pool on the front lawn shows angles gone wavy, blurred by the water. Every pane of glass shines with warm, honeyed light.

"Did you tell them we're feeding a stadium full of people or what?"

Jiyeon reaches out to help balance what Denny is carrying before it can tip over. Their parents have produced a feast which must now be transported into the house via an assortment of containers. "In a way, Eunjae and his brothers count as a stadium full of people. Especially if we're talking about food."

"Jesus," her brother grunts back. "You're right."

The front door is wide open. Jeannie totters inside, a rice cooker in her arms. It's the big one that Mrs. Han brings to church potlucks. She transfers this to the first person she meets in the foyer, complaining about hard physical labor, and then a gaggle of Apollo members bounces onto the driveway: Namgyu, Kei, Jungwoo.

"Yay, you brought more food! Aww, I'm so hungry."

"This means we'll actually get to eat. Nicky takes forever to cook anything."

"I don't even want any of Nicky's food," Kei says, dreary as a Monday morning. "It looks weird, and he put olive oil in the cake. I'm worried."

Jiyeon is wise enough to hide her amusement. On camera and on stage, Kei is imperious by default. The world knows him as an ice prince with a permanent glower, occasionally doling out smiles tinged with frost. Would his fans recognize him right now? He's so glum, like a preschooler on an endless car ride which will only culminate at a dental clinic.

"Moriyama, what are you waiting for? Go get the rest of that stuff out of the trunk. And bring this buffoon with you, then it's one less trip to the car."

Kei snaps to attention. Here is his other mode, suddenly activated. "Captain! Yes, Captain! I'll grow another arm if I have to, Captain!"

"Aww, I want a third arm. That sounds amazing!"

Denny shoots Namgyu a look. "You don't even know what to do with the two arms you've got. Take it down a notch."

"Ha! That's so true!"

Jungwoo relieves Jiyeon of her burden, which is a platter of Mr. Han's famous lemon bars. "Please tell me they had candles at the store," he murmurs. "Jaehwan would never have forgotten those, and if he finds out..."

"I got some. Don't worry."

"You did? Oh, good!" Jungwoo shouts into the depths of the house. "Kazu-hyung! Jiyeon brought candles!"

"See? Told you it would work out."

"So what?" That's Max, whose voice carries from the same direction that Kazu's did. "You always say it'll work out. Half the time you're just talking out of your ass."

More voices ring out in agreement. Kazu cheerfully threatens to add an eleven mile hike to their schedule for the following morning; this safehouse is just a short drive away from a nature preserve.

"Why can't you just admit that you want us all dead?"

"Waaaah, quit getting on his nerves, I hate hiking, I'm *delicate*—"

There's a tug on Jiyeon's sleeve. And it's embarrassing, really, the way she often forgets what she's supposed to be doing when Eunjae calls her name. Or she'll lose track of what she was saying, her attention snagged on the sound of his laughter in another room. What is she, a besotted teenager? Jiyeon assumed she'd missed the window on that one.

No one can ever know, of course. She has a reputation to maintain, a standard to uphold. In this family, Janie flies high and runs far, impossible to tie down. Denny is the one with all his ducks in a row, each duck tagged and numbered, color-coded and trained to march in formation. And Jiyeon? She's in the middle. You can count on her to be calm and steady, an even number dividing neatly. She fills in where she's needed. That's her role.

Her credibility would take a nosedive if anyone knew what Eunjae does to her pulse. But also, who cares? Here he is. It's his birthday, the first she's ever been around for. Jiyeon hooks an arm around his neck and kisses him hello, quickly, before anyone can see.

"So I hope you like cake," she says, "since I brought one too."

Eunjae's eyes light up. "Two cakes? Not sure how I got so lucky." And then he adds, "This 'two cakes' problem. How long have you been dealing with it? Seems like a regular thing."

"Hey, I asked you which slice I should get. You told me I needed both."

"Because you did need both." He smiles at her. "That's the only problem you should ever have."

"People in general or just me?"

"Ah, just you."

See, this is why random strangers are always crying on him, telling their most personal stories uninvited and unprompted. Eunjae has a way of making you feel as though nobody else in the world exists. He can do it with nothing more than a smile or a glance, and after weeks of observation, Jiyeon has concluded that he doesn't even notice it most of the time. He's just being Eunjae.

She's seen videos of their concerts and events; all the members of Apollo are capable of generating this effect, to varying degrees. For example, Kazu's approach nets him countless marriage proposals, and there should be news bulletins updating the body count every time Jaehwan greets a fan by name. It's the reverse with Max, whose frown seems to be his charm point. Denny just snorts and calls this customer service. But Eunjae listens so intently and responds with such sincerity that you never feel like a mere customer. You're special.

"Stop doing the thing," Jiyeon tells him now. She removes her sandals, adding them to the collection of shoes by the door.

"Stop doing what?"

She gestures at his face. "This. I can't do anything about it right now, Eunjae. It's not a fair match."

"All I'm saying is that if I had one wish—"

"Nope."

"If I had one wish," Eunjae persists, laughing, "you'd have no problems, just cake." He pauses. "Maybe not cake, since you'd rather have pie."

"Hmm. I would rather have pie." It's tough, sometimes. Other girls are allowed to be smitten with this man in public and Jiyeon is not. She's supposed to be chill. "And don't use your birthday wish on me."

"Sorry, but I think I will."

Jiyeon has to laugh. The delivery of this sentence is so pleasant and yet so obstinate at the same time. "Fine, but only because two cakes means two wishes. You can use the other wish for yourself. Pick something crazy, okay? It's not too late to start living."

"Not too late for what?" Mrs. Han asks in Korean. She pats Eunjae on the cheek as she walks by. But then she comes back, seizes both of his hands, and cries out, "Late! Oh, that's what I was supposed to tell you. Your birthday gift, it's late! So it's still your birthday when you come back, okay?"

"But you didn't have to get me anything," Eunjae rushes to say. For a second there, Jiyeon thinks he might start apologizing for his own birthday gift.

"Of course we did. Yeonnie, how can he tell me this? Talk to him. He's confused about birthdays."

"Late," Denny says as he strides past them, off to patrol the perimeter. "My bad, Ryan. I had a guy for this and he failed me. On the plus side, now he owes me another favor. It balances out, yeah?"

Mrs. Han concurs. "Late is okay. Late is not the same as never!"

Then Kei comes through the door with Namgyu, lugging the four cases of soda that Mr. Han got for a steal using coupons that morning. "Never too late!" he sings out, inspired by the conversation. Some complicated footwork is executed. More verses follow, the house ringing with song. *Call me and I'll be there*, Jesse sings back to him. And then Jungwoo joins in with, *It's never too late*.

That's from their newest album, Jiyeon belatedly remembers,

as Namgyu belts out the rest of the chorus. He holds the last note for so long that Denny turns back to issue an ominous warning about oxygen deprivation and its effect on the human brain. Nicky shouts from the kitchen that there's no brain in there, Chief, so it's fine. No one laughs louder at this statement than Namgyu himself.

Their hearts are so light, this evening. It lifts Jiyeon's spirits.

"Mr. Birthday Lion Boy!" bellows Mr. Han. He thumps over to Eunjae with an envelope. "Mail for you at the shop today!" It's the right size and shape for a birthday card, one corner taken up by foreign stamps.

Eunjae reads the sender's name. "Oh, from Ezra. He asked where to send it and I gave him that address. Wasn't sure where we'd be, and Denny thought it would be better not to use Ivy Lane."

"Oh, sure. The mail could fall into enemy hands. Den's always going on about that." Jiyeon peeks at the card. Ezra's handwriting is very neat. Did Eunjae's parents remember his birthday? She's afraid to ask. Now is not the time to fly to Australia and ask some very pointed questions of certain individuals.

Despite the size of this house, most everyone has congregated in the formal dining room. It's like something out of a magazine, replete with a sculptural light fixture and floor-to-ceiling windows facing the back garden. The walls are papered in a bold, graphic print that Denny denounces as 'needless frivolity' at least once a day.

Since the table can't seat more than six, Max, Kei, Jesse, and Jeannie end up perched on bar stools, towering above everyone else. Namgyu's on an exercise ball. This seems like a catastrophe waiting to happen, but he's so thrilled about it that no one objects. Nicky opts to eat standing up, since he keeps walking back and forth to the stove anyway. He might be done cooking in time for Eunjae's next birthday.

Jiyeon has eaten with the members of Apollo plenty of times over the past few weeks, but she might never stop marveling at the way they behave during meals. Just as clothing is passed between brothers with little regard for ownership, along with shoes, accessories, and assorted toiletries, there is an unspoken policy that everyone's plate is fair game. No borders exist between place settings. It's like stealing the food improves the flavor.

"Did they all come in this morning, then?" Jiyeon asks Eunjae, leaning close so he can hear her over the din.

"They did," Eunjae replies. He doesn't even react as Jungwoo reaches sideways to pluck a bite of steak from his plate. ("Ari-yah, I'm having a little of this, thanks!") "Just like every year."

He told her yesterday that in addition to the usual seaweed soup, Apollo maintains a birthday tradition of piling into the celebrant's room at the crack of dawn. No one is allowed to sleep in as a treat. Noodles are the mandated breakfast, for a long life. Zero noodles can be left in the bowl. It's an enforced rule.

"One year Max thought he'd be smart and lock his door, but Jaehwan started taking the knob off with a drill."

"Oh, goodness."

"He's nuts, right, noona?" Max calls to her from the other side of the table. "Just plain batshit. Shows up on your birthday like, 'Eat your fucking noodles. You'll live until I say you can stop.'"

"Leader-hyung never lets us do anything. We can't even shorten our lifespans if we want to." Jesse smothers her in a hug. He smells expensive, but also faintly like cake batter. "I live in a jail, noona. I'm *oppressed*."

Kazu rises from his seat in order to put more dishes in front of Jiyeon, scolding the whole time. "Don't talk about Hwannie like that. You'd be running laps on your birthdays if I got to decide."

"Wooooorst."

"Like you even remember our birthdays!"

"He forgot my birthday in 2019! Haha!"

"You do what I do, Kazuhiko," Mrs. Han puts in, sagely. "Just remember the month. Yeonnie? Birthday's in January. So starting January 1st, I say every day, 'Happy birthday, Yeonnie!' Say it all month! Then you can't be wrong."

This makes Eunjae laugh. "Now I know why she's been telling me that since July started."

Kei sidles past, aiming for Namgyu's bowl of kimchi-jjigae. ("I just really feel like something normal. Didn't Nicky cook anything normal?") Mr. Han bellows at Denny as if they aren't right next to each other, and Jesse hops down from his bar stool to swipe some of Jungwoo's salad. ("Lemme have some of your sad food, hyung.") Crunching on lettuce like an overgrown rabbit, he tells Jeannie, "And I told them she was *that* Emma Han, but guess what?"

"They acted like you were crazy, didn't they? That's what happened to me! I said he looks just like Ari from Apollo —"

"Jeannie has a good brain," exclaims Mr. Han. "And good eyes! I've been telling her this!"

"Uncle Joey, please stop spreading this rumor about me," comes the predictable response. "If you have a good brain then people make you use it. I don't get a big enough paycheck for that. And my holiday bonus is paid in bubble tea."

"One," Denny booms at Jeannie, "check your pay stubs. Two, you asked to be paid in product. That's enough rigmarole, Vho."

Jiyeon takes a sip of water. "Rigmarole?"

"You know what I'm saying!"

Out of the blue, Nicky's chopsticks swoop down to claim some more of Eunjae's dinner. "You try this with the sauce yet, Ari? It's good, right? Oh damn, it is. I'm amazing."

"You really are."

Since all chairs are occupied, Nicky plops down in Eunjae's lap. Another brother might evict him instantly, but of course this one doesn't. "And how are *you*, ajumma?" He's got one hand encased in an oven mitt and the other on top of Jiyeon's head, as if conferring a benediction. "Got anything good for me? What's the gossip?"

"Ajussi," Jiyeon replies, "I already told you. Try me on Thursday when Golden Grove comes out for mahjong night. They only have the most dramatic grannies living at Golden Grove. It's like a requirement."

"Ajussi!" crows Namgyu. "Haha, you deserve that one, Nicky."

Just like a textbook Asian uncle, Nicky musses her hair,

delighted. Eunjae nudges the hand away. "Quit, hyung."

"Why? Did you think her hair looks nice? Was I ruining it?"

"It always looks nice," comes the reply, "but let her eat."

"I will, I will. Don't be so scary about it." Nicky addresses the table at large. "Hey, have you guys seen this ajumma's Kazuhiko impression? It's so good. She's my pride and joy." He grins at her. "Come on. Real fast."

"Sure." That one's easy. Jiyeon adopts a lazier posture. She reaches for the buttons on her shirt.

"Yeon-ah."

She looks over to find Eunjae peering at her from behind his brother. "Hmm?"

"What are you doing?"

Jiyeon blinks at him. "He said to do the Kazu impression." She has to raise her voice over a torrent of raucous laughter from everyone else in the room. "Oh, you can't see very well. Ajussi, get off him."

"Ah, that's not it—"

Is he okay? He looks a little flushed. Of course, it's a lot warmer in here thanks to the number of people gathered, so that might be it. But then she realizes what the problem is. Jiyeon reaches around Nicky, who is very busy laughing himself into another plane of reality. She gives Eunjae a consoling pat on the arm. "Sorry," she says. "I'll just do two buttons, not all of them. Don't look so worried. Close your eyes if you have to."

Nicky slides off Eunjae's lap and onto the floor, howling. Since he's out of the way, Jiyeon takes the opportunity to transfer the rest of her own steak to replace what Eunjae lost earlier. Goodness, is everyone okay? She didn't even do anything yet.

It takes a millennium for the uproar to die down. Even then, Kei berates Kazu for at least ten extra minutes. "This is because you can't keep your damn clothes on. It's embarrassing! How do you live with yourself? This idiot said, 'Ohoho act like Kazu,' and the Captain's sister went straight to disrobing—"

Jungwoo hangs his head, shoulders shaking with mirth. "Disrobing. Did you have to use that word?"

"Why are you so mad? Are you just jealous? If you want a body like mine, then go hit the gym—"

"A body like yours!" Jesse screeches, covering Jeannie's ears. "Oh my gosh, Zuzu! She's only eighteen, we're *babies*, you can't talk like that in front of us!"

Even Eunjae has to stop blushing long enough to laugh. He grabs the communal pitcher and refills Jiyeon's water glass. Then, having noticed Max has moved on to dessert, he stands up and carves a corner off his brother's lemon bar with a fork that was supposed to be Nicky's. After chewing thoughtfully for a moment, he gives Mr. Han the most enthusiastic double thumbs up she's ever witnessed. And for some reason, the sight of this makes Jiyeon want to burst into tears.

He leaves next week. They'll all go back to Seoul for two months, maybe even three. Is the summer really over?

The seventeenth of July used to feel so far away, shimmering beyond the horizon like a distant star. Wasn't it still June, just hours ago? A Wednesday night, and Denny's birthday instead.

She'd spotted Eunjae standing in front of the shop in that blue twilight just after sundown, staring at the door as if under a spell. Tall and lithe, hands in his pockets, an easy laugh. And he had a sweet smile, but it always faded far too soon.

The clothes, the contacts, the accent. *What's the story here?* she'd wanted to ask. He wasn't one of their regulars; Wanna Waffle derived most of its business from repeat customers, so Jiyeon noticed new faces right away, despite not being around as much as she used to be. And his eyes were a shade of violet that Jiyeon's twelve-year-old self would've chosen for her bedroom walls. Amethyst Shores, it might have been called, or Lavender Rhapsody, pulled from one of those paint chips at the hardware store. A color for diaries with locks and tiny keys.

Sometimes, in odd moments, Jiyeon's brain still loops itself back to one of the most nonsensical thoughts she's ever had: this guy can't be real. She remembers sitting across from him that night, watching him eat that very first waffle, and beneath all those layers of exhaustion was a face so handsome that someone surely invented it. This was a boy you would write about in your little purple diary. He'd walked right out of a book or a movie. Why wasn't he dreaming still, hidden in the heart of some wild wood?

Jiyeon had invited him in for Waffle Wednesday, driven by some impulse she couldn't name. It might have been the slump to his shoulders. More likely, it was the way he gazed at their orange door with such reverence, as if he'd found some long lost, beloved thing. As if, somehow, he'd found his way home.

She used to play this game with her sister. When their parents bought the shop, Janie was nineteen and Jiyeon was fifteen. Bored to tears behind the counter on those slow summer weekdays, especially in the afternoons, they would people watch to pass the time. They'd make up stories about the customers, when they had them, and anyone walking by outside. But it wasn't merely about inventing lives for people they didn't know. Janie insisted that there always had to be one good thing in every story. She could spot a silver lining from ten miles away, and if no lining existed, she'd spin one out of empty air.

To play the game by Janie's rules, you had to include something for the stranger to look forward to, something amazing that was about to happen to them or might be happening already. And she never cared a whit about plausibility, either. It could be as whimsical as you wanted.

Something good, every time. It counted even if it was small, because things weren't always good back then, and it could be difficult to think of ideas. Jiyeon came to find comfort in dreaming up happiness for other people, what with all the strained whispers between her parents as they closed out the register every evening, and Denny coming home from school with some new scrape or bruise just about daily. She'd learned not to ask about any of it.

Rather than asking, Jiyeon taught herself to retell and reframe. Mom and Dad were just worried they'd miss their favorite show if they took too long to count the money in the till. Denny got that bruise during a spirited dodgeball game. The other kid apologized right after. She wouldn't find herself wanting to storm the office at Lemon Grove Junior High, demanding an audience with the principal. Her little brother had lots of friends. Her little brother was fine.

Janie excelled at coming up with something good. Jiyeon always wanted to match her in every way, but she wasn't as quick to find that flash of silver; her brain always wanted to cut straight through to the problem at hand. She practiced, though. It became easier and easier to bypass her own wiring, to take reality and transmute it into something warmer and kinder.

Emma is dormant now, the name reduced to a coat shrugged on and off, but Jiyeon retained the skills that made her other self so successful: retell the story, reframe it. Your botched hair color isn't a tragedy, it's an opportunity. An adventure. This hair spray? Don't think of it as expensive. It's an investment.

There came a time when she realized that she'd played the storytelling game with her own life a little too well.

That life Jiyeon invented for Eunjae the night he appeared on their doorstep, the name she gave him — it went beyond retelling and reframing. It wasn't a story by Emma Han, curator of fictions great and small. Emma had no part in it. Just Jiyeon trying to find something good. Maybe there's some power to it after all, as Janie would often insist. Now Eunjae is here and part of the story has come true. He's not at the wedding of an imaginary sibling, but he's still at a party, surrounded by people who love him.

She can't cry on his birthday. He'd be so upset. Jiyeon refocuses on the present as Namgyu clangs his spoon against an empty beer can. "When are we singing? Is it time to sing?"

"When is it not time to sing?" Denny mutters to himself.

"Haven't you *been* singing, Hong? When do you ever stop?"

"Gyu's right, though. We should do it now."

"Where's your tablet then? Didn't you say you found a piano app?"

Kei looks at Kazu like he's nuts. "Listen to this old man. I didn't say that, Jesse did!"

"Sorry, sorry. You're all so damn annoying that you start to blur together in my mind."

"Waaah! I'm telling Jaehwan-hyung you said that!"

"Go ahead," Kazu replies. "Hwannie knows you're annoying."

"Waaaah, mean! The meanest dad! Why can't you just be rich? Why do you have to be mean, too?" And then, in English, "Pick a lane!"

Brothers disperse in different directions. Jiyeon looks to Eunjae, who explains, "It's the other birthday thing that we do. A song. I think we started doing that in... 2016, maybe?"

"You guys have a special birthday song?"

"Yeah. Jungwoo wrote it. It was supposed to go on our second album, and we put it to the board as a possible title track, but they wanted something different."

Jungwoo scratches his head, chuckling sheepishly. "It was too sentimental, they told me. Didn't fit the Apollo brand."

"To fit the Apollo brand," says Max, taking a massive bite out of his third lemon bar, "we needed songs that made us sound like asshats."

Jungwoo clears his throat. "Like I was saying, it wasn't what they wanted. I had to try another angle."

"Aww, he was super sad," Namgyu tells Jiyeon. "Me too, though! It's a good song. I love it so much."

"All Apollo songs are good songs," huffs Mr. Han.

Kazu says, "That happened close to Jungwoo's birthday. Ari thought he'd cheer up if we sang it to him, so that's what we did. And now we sing it for everybody's birthday, every year."

The younger three shove a tablet in his face. There's a row of piano keys on the screen, and Kazu coaxes a melody out of them, grumbling a bit when he learns that Jesse paid $2.99 to remove ads. ("Are you kidding me? You know how many other things you could buy for three bucks?") Jiyeon smiles at Eunjae. "What a good idea."

"It really is a great song. We didn't end up using it on any of our albums, but that's fine." He smiles back at her. "This song is ours. It's special, you know?"

Jesse pounds on the table, providing a climactic drumroll to go with his announcement. "Ahem! It's time! Hana, dul, set —"

"Shine bright, it's Apollo!" the others finish automatically. They also bow from wherever they are, with a seamless level of coordination that Jiyeon is still getting used to.

"It's our Ari-hyung's birthday," Jesse says then, deploying what his brothers like to call his variety show voice, "so here we are again with the 2016 hit that never was: *Not Asking Much*."

Where has Jiyeon heard this tune before? She listens, translating the Korean lyrics in her head. It's a slower tempo, but there's something about it that recalls another Apollo song, even if she can't put her finger on it. Maybe it's only that Jungwoo wrote this, and so a common thread runs through. But that doesn't seem like the answer, either.

One more turn around the sun
Four more seasons come and gone
Blossoms drifting down the street
Summer nights arguing on the roof
I've lived another year with you
I'll take another year with you

Eunjae and Namgyu split the chorus and Jiyeon stops trying to figure it out. It really is familiar, like an echo coming from a direction she can't name, but that riddle can wait. She loves to hear Eunjae sing. It never gets old. And he always seems happiest in moments like this one, performing without Apollo's usual slick production and choreography, when he's singing just to sing.

Hey, I just want all of your time
I'm not asking much, I promise
Hey, you can have all of my time
Let's lose count of all the days
It's okay, just stay with me

The boys finish another verse. Eunjae comes in again for the bridge, and then the chorus repeats twice with slightly different words each time. Mrs. Han's eyes are wet above the rim of her water glass. Denny is frowning so hard that there can only be one explanation for it: the song is getting to him, too.

No, it isn't much like the songs that are considered iconically Apollo, the songs that anchor their extensive discography, but Jiyeon can't help feeling that this one is more true to who they are. It isn't too sentimental, whatever the board might have said in the past. Nothing so reductive as that. It's hopeful. It's warm. It's eight brothers piled on top of your bed at daybreak, cajoling you into eating a bowl of noodles. You're young, you feel like you'll live forever, but you clean that bowl. You don't leave a single noodle.

The song winds down. Jeannie and Mr. Han are demanding an encore as soon as the final notes roll out of Kazu's makeshift piano. There's an explosion of birthday greetings from all corners of the room.

"Nice, Keiichi. I'm glad you got Hwannie's lines. That was great."

For once, Kei replies to Kazu without the customary barbed glare. "I've always wanted to sing his part. I wish hyung could be here, though."

"Almost ten years. Soon we can say we've had ten birthdays with each other." Kazu sniffles a little and four brothers are on top of him in an instant, crowding his chair, attempting to climb onto his shoulders.

"Dad's losing it."

Max shoves the whole pitcher of water at him. "How much wine did he have?"

"Aww! Zuzu, you want us to call your mom?"

Meanwhile, Jeannie twists the end of her ponytail around two fingers, brow furrowed. "But why did that sound like *Blame it on Me*? I mean, it's slower and the words aren't the same, but it's so similar."

"Wooooooooow!"

"She caught it!"

Impressed with Jeannie's detective skills, Jungwoo picks up his guitar. Like his notebook, it's usually somewhere within reach. The two things he went out of his way to pack, flying out from Seoul at the last minute: this guitar and Eunjae's camera. Jiyeon thinks this says a lot about Jungwoo as a person.

"Gyu," he says now, strumming a chord, "do the chorus for *Blame it on Me*." Namgyu obliges, happy as a clam. He leaps to his feet and allows the exercise ball to drift under the table. Hand on his heart, he sings:

Baby, let me waste your time
I'll pay it all back, I promise
Hey, I just want all of your time
Let's be late for everything
It's okay, blame it on me

"Huh," mutters Denny. "Maybe I'm having a seizure."

Max rolls his eyes. "Jungwoo had to dumb it way the hell down so the board would take it as a title track. That's how we got *Blame it on Me*."

"Sorry the lyrics aren't intellectual enough for you,

Maximillian."

"Sorry the lyrics are exactly as intellectual as you are, Nicholas."

"Aww! Jungwoo writes the songs of the people! They have universal appeal!"

Eunjae turns to Jiyeon, laughing. "Did you like it?" he asks. "Our birthday song."

"Uh-huh," she replies. "Sing it for me again, sometime."

"Oh my gosh. Ohmygoshohmygosh." Jesse leans forward, grinning from ear to ear. "Noona, can he waste your time?"

Jeering ensues. Max topples him from the bar stool in retaliation. Jiyeon is relieved that the chaos does so much to obscure her feelings. This isn't how you celebrate a birthday, tears in your eyes, everything bittersweet in your mouth. She forces herself to get up, joining Nicky in the kitchen so she can help with the candles. They decide to bring both cakes in together, and a tub of ice cream, but Nicky insists on Jiyeon going first.

"He might do something embarrassing when he sees you," he informs her. "I need that footage. I need it like I need air."

They come to a halt in front of the dining room doors. Double French doors, set with squares of frosted glass. Beyond them, the clamor of voices has died down to an expectant hush. "Give me that," Jungwoo says. He's the blurred shape right next to Eunjae. "I'll do it for you. Don't watch this through your phone, it's important."

"I know," Eunjae replies. "That's why I want to remember it. Hey, not that angle. Hold the phone up higher." A beat passes.

"No, hyung. Tilt it down more."

"Did they already know you're a backseat photographer?"

"Why can't you get anything right, Jungwoo?" Nicky inquires over Jiyeon's shoulder. She's learned that closed doors are no obstacle for him whatsoever. "Is this how you lost your hot actress girlfriend to some American boy—"

"Fuck right off, hyung!"

"Max, you are a very sweet boy," Jiyeon hears her mother saying, "but why is your mouth like this? Your mommy and daddy, they know you talk this way?"

Denny's voice cuts in. He's on standby, prepared to pull the doors open. "Don't wait for them to shut up, Yeonnie. Critical error. That's how we lose agents in the field."

"Waaah, I don't want to be lost in the field, just come in now!"

Still, she hesitates. Nicky peers at her. "Ajumma. Don't do anything embarrassing without giving me a ten second warning. I need that footage, too."

"I'm fine," she answers. Jiyeon takes a breath, then counts to three. When the doors swing inward, she sees that they've cleared out a space on the table, all the bowls and dishes and half-full glasses shoved to one side. Denny's cut the lights so that the candles have less competition, but everybody's phone is out, recording. Jungwoo has two aimed at Jiyeon as she sets the ice cream cake in front of Eunjae.

It's nothing fancy. She got it out of a freezer in the bakery section at the grocery store. HAPPY BIRTHDAY, RYAN KIM has been scrawled on top of it in a loose, looping script.

Jiyeon had hesitated before telling the lady what to write. Would his actual name be better? But it wasn't so long ago that she came up with a story for someone she'd just met. He grew up in San Bernardino and played weekly tennis matches with his cousin. In that imaginary life, there was ice cream cake at every birthday. It felt like the right thing to put on this cake, even though Eunjae never looked anything like someone named Ryan Kim: ordinary, free of baggage, ensconced in a comfortably mundane life.

If she had one wish, that night in June, it would've been for something good to happen to him. Something kinder than reality. He'd been so reluctant to go. Jiyeon didn't know why, but that part didn't matter if he could just be Ryan — someone whose sorrows would burn away by morning, banished by a good night's sleep.

He's never looked like a Ryan, no. But the thing is, Jiyeon wanted him to. She gave him that name to keep him warm.

Their eyes meet in the half dark. Caught in his gaze, she's suddenly the only one here; they're alone in this crowded room. Once, twice, Eunjae seems poised to say something. But he falls silent every time, and as he drags a sleeve across his eyes, Jiyeon's father gently reminds him to make a wish. "Double wishes," adds Mr. Han. "Lucky boy, our Ryan Kim."

"Lucky is right," says Kazu. He's sounding wobbly. Mrs. Han produces a tissue from her purse and he takes it from her, murmuring gratitude.

Max appears at Eunjae's elbow, swimming out of the dark like a ghost. "Hyung," he murmurs, in what Jiyeon recognizes as his most respectful tone, "make some wishes and blow the candles out before the goddamn house burns down."

"But wouldn't that be so funny?"

Kei loses his temper. "Nicky, seriously. Could you try not being a psychopath for five straight minutes?"

"Sorry," says Eunjae at last, still looking at Jiyeon and no one else. "Can't think of anything to wish for."

She forgets that he's leaving soon. All she knows in this moment is that he's something good. She knew it back then, too. Like the lyrics of a song heard long ago, like the taste of those lemon bars that only ever appear on birthdays and holidays, Jiyeon knew it so soon after she met him, as if recalling an undeniable truth from the depths of memory. It made no sense. It still doesn't. Her parents would probably just tell her that this is how love is. Nonsensical. Worth losing your head over, when it's the right person.

"Ryan. You know that cake is from our whole family, right?"

"Yeah, we're still here? Hello, hyung?"

"I didn't sign up for these feelings," says Jeannie, with a sniffle. "I'm off the clock, I can't even be compensated."

"Awwww!"

Memory may fail her later, detail and nuance eroded by time, but Jiyeon can't imagine being unable to recall this: so many smiles shining from so many faces, and eleven phones recording as Eunjae skips blowing out the candles so he can pull her close, hold her tight. Although she's failed to stop the tears from coming, she hugs him back just as fiercely. Jiyeon has missed so many of Eunjae's birthdays, but it isn't too late to make up for it now.

Retell, reframe. A cake from the grocery store, a name spelled out in shaky cursive. Such small things, but the smallest things can render Eunjae speechless with wonder. Jiyeon could stand to see the world that way more often. She could think of these final days differently. It's true that the summer has to end, just as every season has to end, but it also means the next one can begin. And things are good right now, but it's reasonable to assume that they'll only get better.

Better and better, because this is just the beginning.

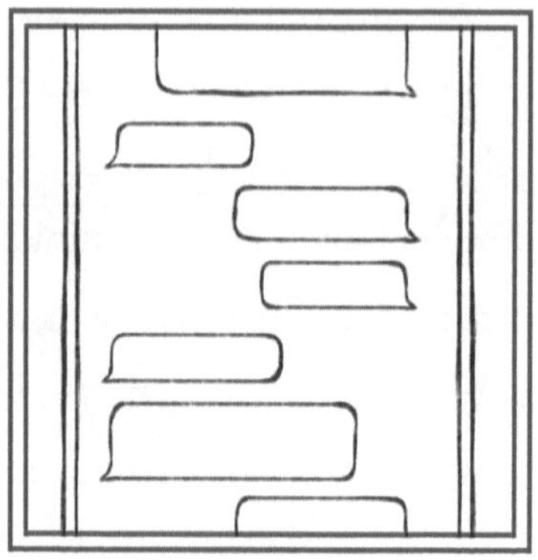

Max: Where's Ari?

Nicky: Ooooh did he run away again?

Jesse: jungwoo-hyung if u dragged him into the woods…

Jungwoo: I didn't drag anyone into the woods! I saw Ari this morning and he was very much alive!

Jesse: waaaahhhh

Jesse: was he alive before AND after u saw him…

Jungwoo: He was fine! Already dressed and everything, that was kind of odd I guess

Nicky: Don't forget that if you need to get rid of a dead body, feel free to do it in full view of Jungwoo between the hours of 6am and 8am during his daily vow of silence

Nicky: He won't be able to yell for help

Jesse: ommggg hyung u still doing that

Jesse: is that why u wouldnt talk to me yesterday morning

Nicky: AND the muse doesn't let him touch his phone until after lunch

Nicky: You'd totally get away with it

Kei: Why do you sound like you're speaking from experience?

Max: So he saw Ari but didn't ask where he was going

Nicky: Wow don't knock his complex creative process

Max: If by complex you mean really fucking stupid

Jaehwan: ???? If it gets me enough tracks for an EP then Jungwoo's creative process can look like whatever he wants.

Jaehwan: And why are you all just sitting around on your phones????

Kei: Because we got ourselves fired… what
  else is there to do?

Jungwoo: Max is just mad that Ari didn't
  tell him where he was going

Max: And you're NOT mad because you don't
  care

Jesse: waaahhh u guys are in the same room
  rn

Jesse: just fight in person

Jesse: dont do it here, why cant we have
  peace on earth while im still in my
  youth

Jungwoo: I'm not fighting with him! He's
  fighting with me!

Kei: The Captain doesn't seem to be worried
  about where Ari went so I think you
  should all just shut up already.

Kei: And anyway the schedule on the fridge
  which all of you can READ says that we
  have free time for another hour. Idiots!

Nicky: Sorry but is that

Nicky: Adrianos, Dark Prince of the Lunar
  Fells???

Jungwoo: Here we go…

Nicky: Farewell fair Lyranel, Princess
  of the Goldenwing Clan!! For I have
  chosen…

Nicky: Another destiny!!

Namgyu: haha!!! well i saw ari in the car with cherished and beautiful jiyeon!

Max: Why couldn't you tell us that earlier??

Jesse: HOW CAN U SAY THIS 2 ME DARK PRINCE ADRIAN WHATEVER THE NAME WAS THAT I FORGOT

Namgyu: we were coming back early and i saw them leaving and i waved but i dont think they saw me

Namgyu: but that's ok!! aww they looked happy

Jesse: ADRIAMOS

Nicky: mY loYaLtY bELoNgS tO tHe CaPtAiN

Namgyu: awwwwww nooooo keiichi went to his room and slammed the door

Nicky: Wait wait okay let's circle back

Nicky: Ari did you elope? What's the scoop my son?

Namgyu: Awwww!!

Jaehwan: Max can elope at any time.

Jaehwan: Consider this my blessing.

Max: Tbh fuck right off!!

Jaehwan: Fuck right off, JAEHWAN-HYUNG.

Jaehwan: Respectfully, JAEHWAN-HYUNG.

Jaehwan: And where the hell is Kazuhiko!

Jaehwan: Why are you all unsupervised!!!!

Jesse: how could ari elope w emma noona without inviting me, i know they didnt do it bc i would be invited…

Kazu: Wait who eloped?? What???

Normal Things

Eunjae

T HERE'S A GARDEN BEHIND this safehouse. Its design is soft, even dreamlike. Against the building's severe geometry, the contrast is twice as pronounced. At first glance, there appears to be no rhyme or reason to the array of grasses and perennials, shrubs and annuals. Wildflowers spill out of beds, dismissive of borders. But Eunjae can see it: the play of colors from one quadrant to the next, and a sense of subtle movement that guides the eye.

He's taken a million pictures. This garden in the morning, when the light is new. This garden in the afternoon, as the sun begins to set beyond the walls. He has photos of the place cloaked in evening shadows, and a few where everything is shrouded in fog, like someone persevered in planting flowers on a cloud. The house is brutal to behold, the furthest thing from friendly, but then this garden offers an embrace.

Since Denny brought them here, Eunjae has often wondered how everything came together with such seemingly artless grace. The designer had to have planned so far in advance. To create this, you would need a grander vision of the shapes and colors that would emerge with the passage of time. There would be a new version of this garden with every turn of the season, built on the versions before it. He wonders what it will look like in the months to come, when he won't be here to see.

Apart from this regret, Eunjae has no complaints. He could admire the scenery indefinitely, stretched lengthwise on the widest porch swing he's ever seen. Jiyeon has fallen asleep with her head tucked into the hollow of his shoulder. She's been there for a while, one arm flung across Eunjae's chest, and he wouldn't wake her for anything. Earlier, he stared so pointedly at his brothers that they took themselves and their constant noise indoors.

The only thing he can do is scroll on his phone, but that's fine. He's prepared to do everything one-handed. His job is to let Jiyeon sleep. Eunjae could stay on that shift for untold hours. When he's tired of wandering the Internet, he can put the phone away and hold her with both arms instead.

Twenty more minutes later, Eunjae's random scrolling has yielded a wealth of information on the area surrounding their current safehouse. Filed under the hashtag for the nearest town, which is called Monroe, he comes across a series of posts announcing local events. It's a busy little town. In the months ahead, there will be a rodeo, a classic car show, and nearly a fortnight's worth of Halloween programming. He reads about a fair they held in the spring. Another fair started two days ago.

He's swiping through aesthetic photos of fruit stands when Jiyeon stirs at last, jolted out of slumber by the sound of Namgyu utterly trouncing Jesse at a board game. She reaches over to adjust the angle on Eunjae's phone, checking the time. "You let me sleep so late," she murmurs, hiding her face in his shirt.

"I did. Don't be mad."

Jiyeon laughs. "I'm so mad." Then she peers at the screen again. "What's that?"

Resting his cheek against the top of her head, Eunjae replies, "The tallest citrus pyramid in California."

"Just California? There's a bigger stack of lemons out there?"

"I know," he says. "I thought the same thing."

"Monroe." Jiyeon swipes through a few more pictures, brow furrowed. "I think we went on a field trip once, in elementary school. A dairy farm or something. It's not so far away from here."

Eunjae looked that up too, while she was still asleep. "Forty-five minutes down the highway." He returns to a post he saved, an ad for the Monroe Township Agricultural Heritage Fair. It's the one that just started two days ago. The caption promises wagon rides and vendors. Framed by balloon arches, the pyramid of bright yellow lemons takes center stage in what appears to be an old airplane hangar. They'll have a food truck serving nothing but pie.

"It looks like fun," he remarks, trying not to sound too

hopeful. He'd like to go, but any outing is risky. Jiyeon might not even be interested. And she's been so tired, taking over for her brother at Wanna Waffle five days a week. He would understand if she wanted to stay home tomorrow. Yesterday, Eunjae got up to help Jungwoo piece together a melody and came back to find Jiyeon asleep on the living room sofa. Kazu was in the middle of tiptoeing away; he'd draped a blanket over her and switched the TV off. Jiyeon slept until dinner, undisturbed.

Now she says, "It does look like fun. Did you see this lemon sorbet? Your favorite." She scrolls down to another post. "They should give their social media manager a raise. I said I'd never take photos in a wheat field ever again, but they made this one look way too pretty."

She sounds so disgusted that he has to laugh. "What made you swear off wheat fields?"

"The ten minutes I spent shaking bugs out of my cute sponsored dress." Jiyeon shudders at the memory, then shows him a post with an event schedule. "Tomorrow's the last day."

"We could go," Eunjae suggests. If she says no, then she says no. He'd be happy to go nowhere and do nothing, if that's what Jiyeon wanted to do.

She smiles at him, though. "Do you want to?"

"Ah, yeah. I really do."

"Hmm. It's my day off. I was gonna get some cleaning done at home—"

"I'll clean," he rushes to say. "Leave me the key. I'll go while you're at work on Tuesday."

"Oh, goodness. It's okay."

"I will. I'm not kidding."

"I can tell," Jiyeon replies, bemused. "Don't worry about it. We can go. I'll just clean on another day, and I bet your brothers would have a great time—"

"They're not coming." Oh, he's interrupted her again. It isn't like him. Normally he'd wait his turn, but it just sort of happened. "Sorry," adds Eunjae, feeling sheepish.

Jiyeon sits up properly. Her face is mere inches away from his, framed by the dark waves of her hair. Is he imagining that the temperature went up a few degrees? Wasn't it cooler just a second ago? They're nearing the end of July, but still.

"You want to go together?" she asks him. "Just you and me?"

He nods. It really is so warm out here.

"So… like a date?"

"If that's okay," answers Eunjae. He doesn't mean to append that upward inflection to the end of the sentence, turning it into more of a question, and it's not a response that will win any awards for eloquence. In the blink of an eye, his assessment of the idea has gone from 'amazing' to 'awful.' Of course she'd be confused; he's in no position to take her out for a day. Eunjae can't even drive over and pick her up. The simplest, baseline elements of a date are off the table when you're 1/9th of a globally recognized idol group. And anyway, what *is* supposed to happen on a date? How did he come up so short on foundational life experiences? He needs to Google this more.

Eunjae is panicking in silence when Jiyeon says, "A date.

We've never done that before. Not officially." Then she covers his mouth with one hand, intercepting what he's about to say next. "No, don't apologize about it. You were going to, I already know. I'm not complaining, Eunjae. There's a lot we can't do and it isn't your fault."

"It is, though," he insists, voice muffled. If it isn't the threat of being discovered, photographed, and exposed to the world, it's the fact that he has seven brothers physically present in the same zip code right now. Well, and Jiyeon's one brother, who counts as nine on multiple levels. But Eunjae feels like the root cause, the one to blame for most of the reasons why they can't just be normal.

Normal. He'd love to be normal, to do normal things. He has a list he keeps in his head, and everything on it qualifies as mundane. For example, who even wants to go to the grocery store? Eunjae does, and not at six in the morning when it just opened, when there's less risk of someone seeing them. He'd like to go get ice cream with Jiyeon, or take a walk. He'd love to run the most boring errands, undisguised, in broad daylight.

He'd love a library card. He'd love an address in a neighborhood within driving distance of her apartment. It sounds so normal, and it seems so far out of his reach.

"It's not your fault," Jiyeon tells him, again. "And if you're sure you want to go—"

"I'm sure."

Joy lights up her face like a sunrise. Jiyeon takes her hand away, leans in close, and kisses him goodnight. Then she's up on her feet, too quick for Eunjae to catch. From the garden gate, she calls out, "Let's go early, okay? I'll let you know when I'm on the way."

Eunjae marvels at how fast she cuts out of there. He stands on the other side of the gate as Jiyeon starts the car, calling to her through the gathering dusk. "Hey, careful going home."

She pops her head out of the driver's side window, still smiling. "See you in the morning." Later, there's a text letting him know she made it back to her apartment, and the second line is this: *Going to bed, then it can be tomorrow!* It's not even 8:30pm.

Something about Jiyeon's excitement makes his chest hurt. Eunjae struggles with the reality that he isn't able to offer her even half of what he'd like to give. He loves that she's so happy to be going. He hates that she must content herself with something so small. But this is the best he can do right now, and it's happening no matter what. Eunjae texts her back, and then he pads into the kitchen to find Denny.

"What, you're asking permission?" Jiyeon's brother grunts at him, once the plans have been explained. "Yeonnie does what she wants." He pulls a cutting board out of a drawer and chooses a knife from the wooden block. "Didn't she take you in right off the street? Like a kitten in a cardboard box. And could I stop her? No. So if my sister wants to go risk life and limb at a farming festival, I guarantee that's what she'll do."

Eunjae nods. These are true statements. The 'risking life and limb' part is distressing, but Denny's always considering every possible scenario. "I just wanted to tell you where we'll be. I didn't want you to worry."

The scowl eases up a bit. "Somebody ought to."

"Thanks for worrying, Den."

"Hmph."

"Do you think it would be okay?" He leans against the kitchen counter, watching Denny cleave a whole pineapple into bite-size chunks, blade flashing like forked lightning. "I'm leaving soon," he says, although it pains him. "I just wanted to have this one day."

Denny sets the knife on the board. He heaves a sigh. "Song Eunjae."

Oh, no. His real name instead of Ryan. Eunjae braces for impact. Did he approach a knife-wielding Denny because he's gotten braver, or because he's grown dramatically stupider?

"Just... watch out for each other, yeah? Pay attention. Stay alert."

"We will."

"*You* probably won't. Someone might as well write 'I'M STUPID FOR HAN JIYEON' on your forehead. I should do it right now."

Eunjae nods again. "If you have a pen, Boss."

Denny's laughter booms through the kitchen. It's dynamite blowing a mountainside to smithereens, or two dreadnoughts trading fire on the open sea, and it's one of Eunjae's favorite sounds in the world. Mr. Han laughs in the exact same way.

"And you're dead serious, too," Denny goes on. "Jesus." Still working through some residual mirth, he returns to his task. "Have fun. Bring me some oranges." *Chop, chop.* "Not those late season mandarins, Ryan." *Chop.* "Valencia or nothing."

"Oranges," Eunjae repeats. "Valencia. Got it."

"Nothing weird will happen as long as you avoid being noticed. Don't do any of the pea-brained things you and the other clowns love to do in public. No sudden dance moves, no tossing your floppy hair every two seconds, and no singing in the middle of the street. Blend in. Dress normal. Be normal."

They hear a distant crash, followed by the dulcet tones of an argument as it gains speed and momentum. Denny crosses to the doorway and roars, "Be normal, for god's sake!"

They set out earlier than early, timing their departure so that younger brothers won't be awake yet and older brothers will still be midway through the morning run. It's only a matter of waiting for Jungwoo to leave with his notebook and a folding camp chair he found in the garage. Sometimes he brings his guitar, too. He's taken to haunting the patch of woodland behind the house, enamored of a creek he found there the day after moving in. This newest songwriting ritual involves vanishing into the trees shortly after dawn. He emerges an hour before lunch, like clockwork.

Eunjae comes downstairs with his camera bag and a baseball cap that might have been his own, originally, until it disappeared on long-term loan. Jungwoo has a rule about not talking for the first few hours he's awake, so they pass each other in the hall with nothing more than a nod and a wave. Eunjae doesn't even have to explain himself.

He hurries through the front door and into Jiyeon's car just as his brother shuffles onto the back patio. Then he buckles his seatbelt, relieved that their escape has gone without a hitch. But then Denny appears at a window on the second floor, sepulchral, an omen of inescapable catastrophe. The sight rattles Eunjae to the core. He fumbles the travel mug Jiyeon brought him, catches it just in time, and almost drops it again despite being in no danger of Denny's wrath today.

Jiyeon doesn't appear to notice. She reverses out of the driveway, humming to herself, and Eunjae endeavors to relax. Instead of glancing back at the house as it recedes behind them, he looks at Jiyeon and can't help smiling. Her mood is contagious.

She catches him looking and smiles back. "Did anyone ask where you were going?"

It takes him a minute to process the question. He responds but immediately forgets what he said. Has he ever seen that dress before? Pale yellow, like sunshine after a summer squall, when the light is soft and clean. A tiny flower winks at him from the ring on her right hand. The outfit is more elaborate than what Jiyeon wears most of the time, now that she isn't working for Olivia anymore.

Eunjae tugs on her sleeve. "You dressed up."

"This is a date, isn't it?"

"But it's too nice. I'm just some guy."

"Hmm. I did hope some guy would think I looked a little too nice today, so it's one goal crossed off the list."

"That's every day," he feels obligated to point out.

"Eunjae, you're being very sweet. Don't make me pull over and do something about it."

He adjusts the vents on his side of the car. Isn't it warm? Why did he think this shirt was appropriate for the season?

The drive is easy, almost a straight shot down the highway. About thirty minutes out, signs begin to appear every few miles, splashed with artistic renderings of oranges and dappled cows. They get so caught up in debating where to find breakfast that Jiyeon misses the exit and has to double back, both of them laughing, Eunjae apologizing for his failure as a navigator. But it's another seven miles down narrow one-lane roads before they reach Monroe, which gives them plenty of time to decide between bakery muffins or diner pancakes.

The decision is made for them when they see the diner shuttered, its charming retro facade marred by planks nailed over every window. The parking lot is piled with cracked tile and stripped flooring. "I guess it hasn't been updated online yet," says Jiyeon. "That's too bad. Cute, isn't it?"

"And the pancakes had great reviews. Here, it's the next right turn and we'll be at the bakery."

She steers the car down a picturesque street and into a shopping center where their destination is flanked by a nail salon and a place selling smoothies. "But this is cute too," Jiyeon remarks. "Everything is so cute. I must not have noticed when I was a kid, on that field trip."

It does seem like a town copy-pasted from a movie. Looking around as they wait in line at the bakery, and then while they follow signs to the fairgrounds, Eunjae is reminded of the stuff his brothers have taken to watching back at the house lately. A marathon called *Christmas in July*, on a channel devoted to nonstop cozy programming. Evenings start out with everybody piled up in front of the TV and end with Nicky or Max getting booted from the living room. They're a little too good at explaining, in sordid detail, how every scene could also work in a horror film.

His brothers. Eunjae had muted the group chat before leaving the house that morning. Against his better judgment, he takes a peek at the messages they've sent. There are immediate repercussions. Eunjae contemplates turning his phone off after the third DID ARI JUST LEAVE US ON READ appears on the screen. Then Jiyeon's phone goes off in her bag.

"Max wants to know where we are," she says, "and Jesse sent a bunch of crying faces. Something about why we eloped without bringing him with us." She starts to type out replies. Eunjae hastens to stop her.

"Ah, what if we put these away? We don't even really need them to take pictures, since I have my camera."

"Oh, sure. I don't mind. But won't they be worried?"

"They'll be okay. I'll text them on the way home."

"Max would say that's really bleeping bleep bleep mean of you," Jiyeon jokes fondly. "You got so bleep bleeping mean, hyung.

Bleeeeep."

He laughs at the sulky glare she's paired with this impression. "Max has Hazel now. He'll understand one day."

"You think they'll stay together? He told me they're breaking up when this is over. Not sure what that means. When what is over? And why are they waiting 'til then?"

"Wish I could tell you. I have no clue. There's some agreement between them and he won't talk to any of us about it."

"Huh," says Jiyeon. "We're kinda boring in comparison, aren't we? Although Jeannie does call it a forbidden romance. No, what did she say last time...?" She thinks, then snaps her fingers. "Forbidden secret celebrity romance. That's it."

Eunjae nearly trips over his own feet. "She's calling it what?" But Jiyeon just pats his arm and tugs him along.

"Come on, Ryan Kim. Let's go find your tower of lemons."

Without the insistent buzzing of new messages coming in, it's easier to pay attention to everything else. It takes ages to make it halfway down the sidewalk; Eunjae keeps wanting to stop and take pictures. Historic buildings line the main street, a parade of dignified brick offices and restored Victorians. On a corner lot is an edifice with Georgian columns, the shutters painted black, window boxes spilling over with snowy white flowers. A brass plaque beside the door says there's a pediatrician downstairs and an orthodontist upstairs.

"Are you a little bit obsessed?" Jiyeon teases him. She's waiting under a light pole hung with yellow banners that flutter in the breeze. Eunjae turns the camera away from the building, frames her in the shot, and takes three more pictures.

"Sorry, sorry. I'm done for now, promise."

Laughing, she says, "I don't mean to rush you, but I was also promised a wagon tour of historic Monroe farmstead. The next one is in fifteen minutes."

"Well, we're not missing that." He reaches for Jiyeon's hand and only briefly thinks about being seen, being noticed or photographed or filmed. It's the opposite of being careful. But the day is beautiful, and she is beautiful, with the summer sunlight shining on her hair.

Jiyeon starts to take his hand, then drops it. "Is it okay? What if someone sees?"

The question reverberates in his head. Why should it even be a question? An ember of defiance grows into a steady flame, fueled by the same sadness and frustration Eunjae felt the other night when she asked other questions just like this one. *I should skip seeing you off at the airport, right? While you're in Seoul, will you still be able to call? Is that allowed?* And the one that hurts the most when he thinks about it: *When will you come home?*

She'd asked out of characteristic practicality. Eunjae would rather not remember, but the day of his departure is close at hand. Soon there will be opposing time zones to coordinate, schedules to line up. She was just trying to get the lay of the land.

The road they've chosen is paved with hard questions. Jiyeon shouldn't have to ask them. She shouldn't have to think twice about reaching for his hand. And even if it's just for now, even if he has to go back to keeping secrets tomorrow, today will be a different story.

"No one will see," he tells her. "It's a pretty big crowd. When we're traveling, sometimes it's easier to avoid being recognized if there's a lot of people around. You wouldn't think so, but that's how it goes."

"I guess they'll be looking at the lemon pyramid anyway."

"And the smaller pyramid made of oranges. Saw them on the website."

She tips her head to the side. "Eunjae, it's very romantic."

"So was the car wash. And the laundromat."

"I liked sitting in traffic with you, too. They say you're a goner but maybe it's me."

What a warm day. Why is it still summer? Do they even have winter in California? When will it cool down?

"Anyway, I'm just trying to say that this is great. I'm glad I get to be here with you. Stop feeling bad, okay? I know you are. I can tell."

There's so much he wants to say. The words won't arrange themselves in coherent order, so Eunjae just offers his hand again. He echoes what she said in the car. "This is a date, isn't it?"

Her smile comes back brighter than it was before. "It is," she answers. They walk the rest of the way down Main Street, hand in hand. Jiyeon asks if it's too soon after breakfast to find the fabled food truck they saw on social media, the one serving pie by the slice. A simple question, one with an easy answer that he's happy to provide.

He was prepared to ward away any curious gazes with

nothing but sheer willpower, but it turns out that Eunjae was right about the crowd. There are many, many more people here than he expected for a weekday in July. It might be because it's the final day. No one reacts to his presence, busy as they are with the sights and sounds of the fair, the friends they've brought with them, the family they're spending time with. He's so grateful he could shout.

The breeze smells like citrus peels and fresh bread. They locate a ring of food trucks, stand in line, and emerge with a huge slice of apple pie and two forks. There's so much hustle and bustle in this area that Eunjae feels safe enough, letting his mask dangle from one ear while he eats. It isn't long before he tucks it into a pocket of his camera bag and resolves to leave it off for the rest of the day. This works out fine, especially as the crowd swells in the afternoon. They're just another couple, one pair out of many, taking selfies and sharing overpriced snacks.

The day passes quickly. Eunjae takes so many pictures that he has to switch memory cards. He reads every printed sign about the area's rich agricultural heritage. He rejects dozens of farm-fresh floral bouquets until the right one turns up, and then he buys it for his girlfriend.

Is there a better life than this? You'd have a hard time proving it to him.

As the afternoon winds down, they jockey for the cheesiest possible poses in front of the lemon pyramid. Jiyeon decides to buy souvenirs for his brothers; she picks out four pairs of fuzzy socks covered in gamboling farm animals and four pairs of sunglasses with lenses shaped like oranges. Eunjae warns her that it's best to buy them all the same thing, since it'll only result in a squabble otherwise, but Jiyeon thinks their bickering is funny and goes through with it anyway.

"Wouldn't it be a fight no matter what you bought for them?" she points out, as they're walking to the car. The sun is setting and Denny has dispatched one terse message to each phone with a reminder that dinner is at 1900 hours sharp.

"Ah, yeah. Just how it goes. I have too many brothers."

"I have too many brothers," Jiyeon replies darkly. "What if I didn't want to eat dinner there today? Why does he get to set a curfew?"

Eunjae is chuckling at this, loading shopping bags into the trunk, when he hears a gasp. It's followed by the drumbeat of sneakers and sandals pounding across the packed dirt of the fairground parking area. His stomach drops. Survival instincts take over — he jams the baseball cap onto his head and snaps the mask back into place. It was too much to hope that his luck would last until they were safely headed home again.

He's expecting to turn around and find a small horde of Sunshines staring at him. Where is Jiyeon? Did she duck behind the car? But it turns out that she's right there, coming around to meet this intrusion halfway. The strangers are in gingham dresses and sprigged cotton blouses. One carries a wicker picnic basket. Another has a pretty serious camera slung around her neck, same as Eunjae. None of them pays him any attention.

"Emma? Emma, it *is* you!"

"Oh, wow. I told you it was Emma Han! I knew it!"

"Yup, it's me," says Jiyeon. The girls come in for hugs like they're old friends. "Were you guys in that field earlier?" she asks them. "I was thinking how brave you were."

"That was Clare's idea." This from the girl with the picnic basket. An Instagram handle has been printed on her camera strap in blue cursive: *@bri_berrie*.

"Our worst ideas are always from Clare. I told Brianna we should just cut and run."

Clare crosses her arms, belled sleeves flapping like flags. "The bugs weren't that bad. And no one told Katie to wear a dress today."

"I had to wear gingham. I have a whole series coming up."

"At least it was a really pretty day for it," says Jiyeon.

"How you been though, Emms?" Brianna inquires. "We saw that post last month."

Eunjae loads up Denny's crate of oranges, trying his hardest to fade into the background. Jiyeon gives all the rehearsed responses about what happened, telling a version of the story that seems informative on the surface but doesn't really divulge anything substantial. She sidesteps the more intrusive questions, friendly and yet noncommittal.

He struggles through what feels like dissonance and clarity at the same time. This is Emma speaking, not Jiyeon. It's not so different from when Ari is speaking instead of Eunjae. He senses the switch, knows her well enough to detect the change. Still, it reminds him that so much remains a mystery. Does she ever feel that way about him?

"But you're coming back, right? From your social media break, I mean."

"Well, yeah," Clare chimes in. To Eunjae's dismay, she looks right at him. "That's Phillip, isn't it? Why would she be out here in the boonies with him if it wasn't for content?"

"I did hear that the event committee decided to invite a bunch of us this year. Wasn't the gift basket adorable?" Brianna shakes the picnic basket. "See? We repurposed it."

But Katie has joined Clare in taking a second look at Eunjae. "Are you sure that's Phillip?"

"Who else would it be? That's definitely not Arthur, they broke up." The girl with the camera wags a playful finger at Jiyeon. "Lots of people were saying you're with someone in that boy band."

"Oh, sure," says Jiyeon. The girls think this is funny and Eunjae thinks he needs to go lay down.

"Hope you've stayed out of the comments. Those fans have a lot to say about you."

"It'll blow over," Katie murmurs absently. "But I met Phillip a couple times and I guess I don't remember him being that tall."

"Where do you keep finding these guys? Send me a Phillip or one of his friends."

"Send me Arthur since you're done with him, Emms."

"That's not Arthur," says Jiyeon, managing to get a word in. "It's not Phillip, either."

Clare squints at Eunjae some more. "Oh, I see," she replies, somewhat embarrassed. "Of course! He's so obviously not the same guy, no idea what I was thinking. It's a new Phillip!"

Jiyeon makes no effort to correct that assertion. Deftly, she maneuvers the conversation down different paths. For the next ten minutes, the talk turns to Clare's clothing collab, changes to the algorithm, and the provenance of Katie's dress. She doesn't allow herself to become the focus of the conversation again. Eunjae dives for the safety of the car. He's a bundle of nerves in the passenger seat by the time Jiyeon joins him.

As soon as she's positive that the other three have drifted away, she takes a moment to rest her forehead against the steering wheel. "Whew. I didn't see that coming."

"You okay?" he asks.

"I'm okay. It was just... weird. I wasn't ready for it." She gets the car started, retracing their route back to the highway. "I was so prepared for someone to recognize you. I didn't even imagine it happening to me instead. What were the odds?"

The lights of the fair gradually vanish in the distance. On the ride home, Jiyeon tells him how they all know each other and from where. But those girls belong to the world she's chosen to leave behind, so Eunjae is careful to listen without asking too many questions. He senses that these would be hard questions. Didn't he promise her, if only in his head, that there would be no hard questions today? As far as he's concerned, that goes for both asking and answering.

There is one thing, though. Just one quick puzzle he ventures to solve, in the driveway as the last safehouse looms over them, windows ablaze with warmth.

"Yeon-ah," he says, nudging her shoulder with his. "Who's Phillip?"

Her eyes are wide when she turns to face him, yellow dress swirling around her knees. "Oh! I didn't realize you heard that part, I thought you were already in the car. I'm so sorry. You must be so confused." But then Jiyeon is clearly fighting an urge to laugh. She wraps both arms around him and says, "Phillip was my photographer."

He wraps his arms around her, too. "Ah. Your photographer."

"Uh-huh. I had a client who taught at this arts college," she explains, "and she asked around for me, to see if any photography majors wanted a part-time gig. I still had to work my day job, cutting hair, but there was always something I had to be promoting. It was taking me hours to put all that content together on my own. Having Phillip was great because I could do a few shoots a week and he'd just follow me around with his camera."

Eunjae contemplates this information. Jiyeon, meanwhile, descends into full-blown laughter. "Oh, Eunjae. I really am sorry. It's so dark out here, and I couldn't figure out if you were mad at me. Were you mad at me? Are you mad at me right now?"

"I'm so mad." His response only makes her laugh more. Jiyeon laughs so much that she even snorts a little, and then he's gone too. He can't pretend to be serious anymore. It's too much. Jiyeon hugs him tight, and he sits back against the trunk of her car while they both laugh until their faces hurt.

"When she asked where you keep finding them—"

"Like I'm getting men out of a vending machine." She dashes a tear from her eye. "I should see how Phillip's doing. He's graduating soon, or just graduated. I bet Denny knows."

"Tell Phillip I want his old job," says Eunjae.

Jiyeon reaches up, her fingers curved around his cheek. Instinctively, he leans into her touch. "You can't take another job," she replies. "You owe me four songs. No, five. I handled that Code Orange for you."

In three days, Eunjae will be on a plane. How is he supposed to leave so soon after finding her?

"Aww, is that them? Are they back from eloping?"

"Noooonnnaaaaaa, what did you bring me? You brought me something, right?"

"Why the hell does she have to bring you anything? Go back inside."

They pull apart as brothers tumble through the gate. The trunk is emptied, its contents whisked into the house to be examined and shouted over, and Eunjae trails behind the others with the camera bag he'd nearly forgotten in the front seat. He glances up to find Jiyeon waiting for him on the path.

Time folds inward, collapsing until this Jiyeon overlaps with the one he first met. There are so many versions of her that he didn't get to know, younger versions he missed and can only encounter through stories. Then there are the versions of Jiyeon he has yet to discover, part of a future he can only imagine.

Sometimes, like right now, he feels the happiness of being with her and the inexplicable sense of having lost her, all at once.

This version of Jiyeon will never occur again. They can't return to this day, this hour, this moment. A camera can only work so much magic.

He's taken a million pictures anyway. Jiyeon in the morning, sitting across from him, going over a grocery list with Denny. Jiyeon from earlier this afternoon, holding up an orange blossom spun from glass. Eunjae has photos of her carrying a birthday cake, photos of her pulling clothes out of an industrial dryer in the middle of the night. But for every version of her that he holds on to, there are more he won't get back again: Jiyeon smiling at him from the doorway at Ivy Lane, and Jiyeon in the diffuse glow of a street lamp, telling him that yes, of course he can stay.

She says his name. The memories recede. Inside, dishes clink and brothers sing along to a holiday song on TV. It's Christmas in July. Eunjae catches up with Jiyeon at the gate. She loops an arm through his, asking if he's hungry, trying to guess what dinner might be. Can she see the pictures he took today? Does he feel like running away again tomorrow? There's another diner on the highway, in the opposite direction. The sign says it's open twenty-four hours. "I had the best day," she adds. "Did you?"

It's an easy question to answer, but the words elude him once again. He kisses her instead. Her arms slip around his neck. There's a gap here between two windows, narrow and thrown into deep shadow; if they stay within this space, no one can see. And this is not a moment he can keep, either. It's a moment to be lost in. They both forget, for a while. In the end, they're late for dinner.

Somewhere in time, is there a version of her still calling

to him from the other side of an orange door? Because Eunjae doesn't know what happens next, but he's sure — so sure — that every version of himself would answer her the same way. He'd go through that door. He'd do it all again.

Eunjae has no grand vision. He just knows which way is home.

ANNA
AFFLE

Acknowledgments

I WOULDN'T BE HERE, writing the acknowledgments of a second book, if not for the readers who took a chance on *This Place is Magic*. Every day, without fail, I'm amazed at the way a book about kind people managed to bring me nothing but kind people in return. Sunshines, I can never thank you enough for all your messages and reviews and photos, for campaigning to get TPIM into libraries and bookstores, for sharing it with friends and family. I followed a boy named Eunjae through an orange door last summer, and what we found on the other side was you.

To the wonderful booksellers who have supported me on this journey, especially Aerie Brown here at Blue Willow Bookshop in Houston, thank you for reading my book and finding room for it on the shelves. You just really have my heart. I couldn't live this dream without you.

To fellow author J Greene: I feel boundless gratitude under foreboding skies full of storm-laden clouds that weep silvery tears on the vast world~

I'm immensely thankful to Enid Din (*@enid.din*) for illustrating such a gorgeous cover for *This Song is Ours*; it's everything I imagined it would be, and more. Readers complain to me that the first book makes them want to eat waffles at 2am, and now Enid did such an amazing job that I'm pretty sure I'll get DMs about craving waffles AND an entire birthday feast at 2am. (Hit me, guys. It sounds like a 'you' problem, to be honest ♥) Enid, thank you for everything!

Joeli (*@joe___lx*) gets her own paragraph, and part of the dedication too, because GUYS. She is my angel on this earth! She works SO hard, I mean you have no idea what an insane taskmaster I am. I have projects lined up to infinity. And no matter what I ask Joey to draw for me, she never tells me to go away and leave her alone. No idea why! She hasn't even given me a mug that says WORST BOSS EVER even though I keep her endlessly toiling on art for this series. Joey, I am so fortunate to have found you. With all my heart, thank you for drawing nine clowns over and over again and making them look absurdly hot at the same time. I love you so much!!!!

It would not be possible for me to pursue so many absolute breadloser hobbies without the support of my husband. If anyone deserves a medal for being patient while I yap about distributors, trim sizes, litigation in the K-pop industry, and the fact that I once again did NOT pull the photo card with my bias on it, it's this man. 10/10, would marry again. And thank you to my 5-year-old for promoting Mommy's agenda by wearing his Wanna Waffle tee without complaining!

Apollo belongs to their fans, but I belong to my investors. Thank you once again to Stakeholders for listening to me talk about my books night and day, every day, all the time. I can aspire to any deranged undertaking and know that these people will support me, pose their cat with my newest merch (Marty, the power behind the throne!), and say so many nice things about my work to random strangers that I need to go lay down. I never have to wonder if I'm loved. This is a gift you're always giving me.

Not everyone can say that their editor is also a beloved friend, a librarian, a phenomenal teacher, a martial arts master, AND Denny's Ultimate Warrior™ because there's only one Carrie and she only edits for me. Sorry! Editor-nim, we love you so much! Thanks for making sure all brothers are accounted for at all times, taking the best #WaffleWednesday photos, and being the best auntie to all my sons, real and fictional.

The last paragraph is always for Ayana, saltmate and Chief Stakeholder, who keeps me chained to my desk and should be the one you bribe if you ever want anything from me creatively. She accepts payment in cash and/or real estate, preferably a villa in Tuscany if you can swing it. Chief, you know every book is for you. It's the least I can do when you've been here for ten years, the first to hear every harebrained story pitch. You're so super unsympathetic when I'm gripped by demonic possession. I write to make you proud — thank you for your unwavering belief in me.

ABOUT THE AUTHOR

Irene Te is a veteran K-pop fan and critically acclaimed author of cozy contemporary stories full of humor and heart. Her debut novel, *This Place is Magic*, was chosen by librarians as the best entry in Contemporary Fiction for the 2024 Indie Author Project and received the Grand Prize at the 32nd Annual *Writer's Digest* Self-Published Book Awards. When she's not writing, Irene works as a freelance curriculum and instructional designer. She lives in Houston, Texas with her husband and son. You can visit Irene at www.irenete.com or connect with her on Instagram (@irenewritesthings).

THANKS
for reading!

P.S. Subscribe to my monthly email for the latest updates and exclusive bonus content, including 2 extra chapters for *This Place is Magic*!

irenewritesthings.substack.com